THE DAY THE CLOUD STOOD STILL

PATRICK TROTTI

The Day The Cloud Stood Still

Published by Ever Books, an imprint of Pteron Press

© 2014 Patrick Trotti

First edition.

Pteron Press, Palermo and Helsinki.

Cover design by Michael J. Seidlinger

ISBN (13): 978-952-6624-21-1

Acknowledgments

An excerpt of this book appeared in the September 2012 issue of Necessary Fiction. Thanks to Nancy Freund for being the first one to see parts of the book and like it enough to publish it.

This book was written in the friendly confines of Coffee Lab Roasters and Warner Library. The large iced coffees kept me charged and the quietness of the library allowed me to complete this project.

I'd like to thank Timo Tuhkanen for his care, guidance, patience, and thoughtfulness throughout this process. Special thanks goes out to the three amigos, Kevin, Ron, and Tom. Shout out to Lena Olive and Austin Islam for their eye for detail when the text needed new eyes to look it over. Thanks to my mom for sending me to Iowa a few summers ago, where I learned the difference between being someone who writes and being a writer.

None of this would've been possible without my dad. Your confidence and dedication sustained me during the dark times and made the good times all the more enjoyable. I couldn't have asked for a better role model. Everything I do is in the hope of making you proud.

"Ever tried. Ever failed.
No matter. Try Again.
Fail again. Fail better."
~
Samuel Beckett

This book is dedicated to my late grandfather who, despite missing the publication by a few months, is definitely reading it from above.

The final pages were written by his bedside in the hospital as he reached out for hugs every few minutes, a smile on his face right up until the end. He was my best friend and the person I respected the most. He taught me what it meant to be a man, about sacrifice and dedication and, most of all, about what unconditional love is all about.

You'll forever live on in my heart. R.I.P.

THE DAY THE CLOUD STOOD STILL

The first flake of snow came in May. We hadn't been warned. It descended upon us by surprise. Mom screamed out to my dad. She begged him to look out the kitchen window, to confirm what she witnessed. I rushed downstairs and joined them, amazed and confused. It was only a few flakes, tiny pieces of dandruff dropped from the sky, but that didn't lessen my excitement. I wanted more. I wanted the sky to open, to dump inches, feet onto our yard.

The earliest storm we ever had was in September. My regular thoughts weren't a concern to me though. The possibility of a day off from school hadn't come to mind. This was special, required me to be in the moment, drowned out my surroundings. I focused on the white bits, tried to isolate them in mid-air, traced their path to the fertile ground.

I stared up into the sky for a few minutes, oblivious to my surroundings. A giant gray cloud hung over me in the front yard. It taunted my smallness. It was a different shade of gray, a deep, sharp color. Almost charcoal, like the stuff that dad produced on the grill while he cursed, as he heaved piles of meat into the trash last summer. Mom called me inside worried about what the neighbors would say.

Dad stayed in the kitchen, unmoved by the freak snow. He waited for dinner in silence. It didn't affect him like mom and me. It was the best thing to happen to me since the day that I stayed home from school at the start of the year with fake stomach pains. The gift for my accomplishment was the porn channel unscrambled on the television.

We didn't have a severe winter, it only snowed a handful of **times, mostly in January. One day of school cancelled, an all time low for** me. This snow, though, was a hint of things to come, a teaser.

The events of yesterday drove me to the window the next morning. The surface was cold. There was no more snow, just remnants of yesterday's surprise. That didn't stop me from going outside for a closer look. Each individual flake had hit the ground and failed to melt away. It refused to vanish; it wanted to make its presence felt. Flecks of white littered the front yard like a confetti bomb had gone off.

Despite all of the excitement, I had to get ready for school. I wanted to stay home, not to miss a test or because of an incomplete homework assignment. This was different; this was something greater than myself. As I changed for school my mind wandered to the potential importance of the snow. It was the timing not the severity that had my attention. If it could just continue to pick up strength, maybe I could get an unexpected day off from school. But that was just wishful thinking.

I licked my thumb while at the bus stop, reached down and picked up a piece. It didn't dissolve on my finger like the snow from past storms. The white speck stayed there, looked back at me as if my touch didn't bother it. It was indestructible; it failed to be flicked off, forgotten.

The sky was still gray, that same cloud overlooked the entire town. The shape remained unchanged. It looked as if it hadn't moved an inch. It had been 24 hours since I'd seen the sun. My eyes weren't acclimated to the dullness. My system was still in shock.

On the bus everyone fought for a window seat. Boys positioned themselves against the smaller girls, boxing them out of a good seat. I found one and pressed my face up against the dirty glass. I felt like a child again, my anticipation for the next moment was at an all time high. The ride to school was quiet and surreal. We remained under the cloud. It was as if we'd traveled in disguise, under a blanket of darkness. There was a collective gasp, an exhale of disappointment, when the bus pulled up to school. The show was over. For the rest of the day we'd be stuck inside, unable to track the mystery cloud.

At school, talk of the snow was everywhere. It started in the high school and leaked down the road to our middle school. In the cafeteria we wondered if it would continue. Most of us held out hope for more snow. We'd convinced ourselves that it wouldn't stop.

Bobby proclaimed the storm insignificant, nothing more than a blip on the radar. His dad worked with weather in some capacity. He was never on the news or in the paper but he still held more authority than our collective wishes.

Another kid at the table scoffed, said that Bobby's dad knew nothing about nothing. Bobby took it as a challenge. He invited us over that afternoon to watch his dad's current experiment. The table fell silent.

"Let's go now," I said.

The piece of snow was still on my thumb. It felt like a piece of ash. The harder I tried to get rid of it, the more pronounced its appearance became. Dad had a similar problem when he got drunk and would clumsily stub out a cigarette in the ashtray, his fingers darkened for the rest of the night.

"You sure about this Wilson?" Bobby asked.

A simple nod was all that was needed.

Bobby's house was a five-minute walk from the school. It was bigger than my house. We entered through the side door, by the garage. I followed his lead, took my shoes off and laid them by the kitchen door and hung up my coat. We didn't speak.

The kitchen was empty of people. Things were piled up everywhere; envelopes and papers of all different sizes dominated the counter.

Baskets filled with elaborate key chains, stacks of cookbooks, even clothes were on the main table in the center of the room. The white refrigerator was filled from top to bottom with pictures and magnets, a web of family history haphazardly connected.

Bobby wasn't ashamed of the mess. He continued through the room and made a sharp left, opened a door and scurried down the steps. I never liked basements. They all had that damp moldy smell. The steps creaked with the weight of each of my feet. The light at the bottom illuminated the rest of the room. It grew in strength by the last step. Bobby stared up at me impatiently.

"Come on, my dad's gonna be home soon."

He was terrified; it was on his face. I recognized it. It was the same look dad gave me any time I snuck into my parent's bedroom and rummaged through his closet in search of his dirty magazines.

My head almost hit the beams above, forced me to duck and slouch to keep my five-foot nine-inch frame unharmed. Bobby, who was five feet tall, had no problems. The wood panels that covered the walls were painted over in an olive green color that looked like a military barrack. The floor was cold. The cement sparkled in the light, which made me feel uncomfortable. My toes grew numb with each step towards the back of the room. My wool socks were in my dresser drawer back home.

On the back wall was a giant wooden table, like the kind you saw on construction sites or in an architect's office. The surface was full of items, which didn't make sense individually. A dirty beaker, a long, skinny test tube. Crumpled up pieces of paper in all shades of colors. Old radios with giant antennas crawled out in every possible direction.

As we got closer more details appeared. Pencils were scattered across the tabletop. They ranged in size from the ones we used for our tests at school to the really small ones they give you at miniature golf. I only played once; my dad took me after he listened to me beg for weeks. We lasted the first four holes before he hit his ball too hard. The ball jumped off the green carpet and rolled out into the woods past the chain linked fence. He got into an argument with the manager when he found out it would cost him an extra two dollars for a new one. My dad cursed at him, dropped his club, and dragged me out of there before I had time to react. My neon yellow ball from that day still is in my room somewhere.

Beyond the pencils, other objects came into focus. There were all of these charts and diagrams underneath the scientific tools. They looked foreign. Bobby probably didn't understand them either. They were filled with long equations, scribbled out mathematical processes that were somehow related to the weather.

On either side of the table were two long bookshelves. They were crammed with textbooks and more of those rolled up large pieces of paper. It reminded me of my friend Joshua's Bar Mitzvah. They looked like those pages that he had to read out loud from, in front of everyone. I stood in the back with the rest of his friends and tried hard not to laugh at his phlegm-riddled stutter. Apparently he had become a man. That was a few months back. It was the only time I'd ever been in a Temple. He's the only Jewish kid I knew.

Each shelf looked as if it took on just enough weight, like if one more piece of paper were placed on it the whole thing would tumble down. The paper was dusty, worn at the edges, discolored from years of existence. Bobby was right, his dad did seem important. How it related to the snow was still unknown to me.

There was one stool, gray metallic in color, at the table. Bobby sat and I stood beside him. I was careful not to touch anything despite my urge to shake it up, pour stuff, and watch things change color. As if this would somehow explain the snow.

"I told you," he said.

"Told me what?"

"That my dad is important. He's down here every night working on this stuff. He even sends out his findings in the mail every few weeks to some office in California."

Bobby turned in his stool, looked right at me and waited for a response. His eyes were bigger now, excited with his own exaggerations of his father's significance.

"Wow, well do you know what any of this stuff means?"

Bobby sat in silence. He was the smartest kid in our grade but he was stumped.

"No, that's my dad's job. But sometimes he lets me help him."

"Cool," I said.

The same address and last name was the extent of what was shared between my dad and me. We had nothing like this, not even close.

The radio on the table started to buzz. It broke up the silence between the two of us, sounded like a mixture of a weather report and a warning. It was muffled, barely audible. We both leaned in. The voice didn't sound familiar but the way that this unknown man pronounced every syllable, took a deep breath in between certain key words for effect, drew me closer. By the end of the second sentence we were so close that our eyelids were up against the dials. Bobby coughed and I nudged him to stay quiet, to listen. This was better than the beakers and tubes and drawings.

'Outlook is grim, very grim…Take shelter and wait for further in-structions…This looks like it will last a long, long time…The only thing you can do now is…'

Then static. Bobby picked up the radio and shook it in his feeble hands. He put it down and played with the dials. He was eager to hear the rest of the instructions, of what we could, should, do. The static grew louder as the two of us stood there, anxious for some kind of return. There was some laughter in the background below the surface of the grumbled noise from the radio. I pictured some older ham radio operator in his parents' basement content with the confusion he created. It worked. Maybe it was a stupid prank? Bobby couldn't be sure either. After five minutes Bobby sat back down on the stool. His legs shook, hands trembled. He looked up at me. He wanted to say something important and smart to rationalize what we heard. His mouth was open but, like the radio, there were no words.

Movement from above interrupted the silence. We could hear foot-steps; they came from the main floor.

"Shit, we gotta go."

"What? Why?"

"My dad's here. Follow me," Bobby said.

He zipped up the steps in a few long strides. We both made sure to be as quiet as possible. The noise came from the second floor as we reached the top step. Bobby looked back at me, eyes panicked. It was the same look that was plastered on my face that first time I found the good pages of my dad's collection and heard him open the front door downstairs.

"Get your stuff and go. I'll see you later."

Words of encouragement rang through my head. Thank you, don't worry, stay calm, it's no big deal. Nothing came out. Instead I nodded, slipped my shoes on, grabbed my jacket, and headed out the side of the house and onto the street.

We'd spent an hour in his basement, which meant school had ended. The walk home was slow. I snuck in unnoticed, went straight upstairs to my room, and locked the door even though dad's number one rule in the house was no locked doors.

That night, busy with homework about the Roman Empire, the snow began again. There were no shouts from my parents. This time the snow fell by itself. There were more of them; individual flakes that were feet apart the first time were now within a few inches of each other. They were bigger, denser, as they hit the ground with a dull thud instead of a feathery silence.

The weather was just another diversion. My mind, regardless of the distraction, remained on the scene in Bobby's basement. To what we saw, to what we heard, to what I heard afterwards. It was possible that we heard a part of a conversation, out of context, that wasn't meant for us. Maybe we wanted some mystery to surround the whole thing. The idea of no concrete answer terrified me.

Everyone was slowed by the weather. People moved in short bursts. They looked to be stuck in quick sand. The weather had a different effect on me. It had awakened something. The cold flakes coursed through my blood, made me feel alive for the first time in years.

I went outside for lunch, alone, except for my peanut butter and jelly sandwich and kicked together some flakes, formed a pile at the end of the playground. It wasn't much but the prospects of future snowball fights increased with every flake that fell.

The second half of school went by in a blur. The flakes reappeared by final period. Stray flecks of grayish white accompanied each fact recited by my teacher. The snow fell with more intensity by the time we boarded the bus. It had become wet and heavy; hit my shoulder with a thud. Marked its territory one drop at a time.

By sunset the temperature was in the low twenties. Excitement at the promise of tomorrow morning kept me from sleep. It felt like Christmas Eve when Santa Claus was still real. One last look out my bedroom window found that the storm had gained momentum. The flakes whirled by the streetlights in clumps. They blocked out the dull, neon light. It was quiet outside by the time I fell asleep. No cars were on the road. The endless buzz of the trains that rumbled through our town even came to a halt. All that was left was my imagination and the faint murmur of nature as it took over and dominated the night.

School was closed the next day, which gave me the rare chance to watch television and eat in the living room. There were no rules really, just stay out of trouble. Both of my parents stayed home from work. Mom called the diner where she waitressed and asked for someone to cover her shift. Dad was on the phone for an hour with his boss from the factory. Nobody liked him. Dad never said anything nice about him. He always made him angry and left him in a bad mood, which dad took out on us.

Dad kept me locked inside, fixed on the television screen. I'd have to wait to venture outside. He'd taken away the controller. No more action movies. We watched the local news. Around the clock coverage of this "weather phenomenon" as they called it. By mid day both of my parents were in a trance. They drooled over morsels of information already told to them the previous hour. Snowfall totals were regurgitated with the same zeal as last year when they covered the Presidential election. Every detail mattered. The sun hadn't come out in three days. We'd gone through dreary stretches in the past but never before had it been this unexpected.

"Bobby told me that his dad said this was a temporary thing. He's a real smart guy. Probably smarter than these weathermen," I said.

"That's not saying much. They're wrong half the god damn time."

"That's not the point. Bobby's dad…"

My dad cut me off, but continued to stare at the screen.

"Bobby's dad is a freak. He's an accountant, not a scientist!"

"There's hope though, right?"

"Hope is made up. Don't exist, at least not in this town," he said.

"I know what we saw."

"What did you say?"

"His dad's basement was filled with stuff. He had all this equipment. Very technical stuff," I said.

"No more! You hear me? He'll fill your head with crazy ideas."

He got up from his recliner and fetched another beer from the fridge. He returned and stood there for a moment. I didn't want to get him angry. His mood changed easily. Now, with the storm, there was no escape.

Standing there he looked like an older, out of shape offensive lineman. Inside the house he looked comical, like it had been built for someone half his size. He always banged into things; hand on his head as he cursed at inanimate objects. Mom said it was because of all the beer he drank.

Before he finished his next beer he stepped towards the window. He looked outside and surveyed the damage so far. His hair blended into the backdrop outside. Spots of dark black clashed up against patches of white and gray that covered much of his head. He looked like a fat raccoon.

"But he wasn't even there! It was Bobby and me."

"That's even worse. No good comes of kids fucking around with grown up shit. You hear me?"

I sighed and shrugged. Hoped my vagueness would suffice. It didn't.

"I'm warning you," dad said.

He stepped towards me; his dark brown eyes trained on me like an eagle. The house shook as he stomped his boots for effect. It was my cue to drop the argument.

"Fine, I won't go over there."

By late afternoon the news had shifted. Nowhere outside of our town limits had a drop of snow been recorded in the previous three days.

We were in an "extreme weather zone." They used words like isolated, severe, and unprecedented.

A reporter, puffed up in his parka jacket, struggled to hold on to the microphone with his oversized gloves. He wasn't prepared for this. Neither were we as we watched in short sleeves and shorts. They cut to a commercial. Teased us with this man in the elements. Mom went up to the attic to bring down a few boxes of winter wear.

"Just in case this continues," she said.

In less than seventy-two hours this snow had become a thing, gained life. It was a form that preoccupied all of the adults in my life.

The reporter reappeared on the screen after a commercial for a summer water park nearby. He struggled to stand his ground as the wind picked up. He was at the town limits. I could make out our town's welcome sign over his shoulder. The hardwood sign that symbolized our town's work ethic was filled over with frozen ice. Behind him, off in the distance, kids got off of a school bus, met by their parents. Hordes of minivans waited in a row on the side of the dead-end street. The kids wore t-shirts and shorts; sandals covered their feet. The reporter stopped mid-sentence, turned and marveled at the oddity. He stepped over the border to the next town and tried to get a quick interview with a family. Beads of perspiration dripped down his forehead by the time he reached one mother. Sweat trickled onto the microphone.

"I'm here live with Mary, whose son attends Salem Central Middle School. Mary let me ask you, what do you make of this whacky weather?"

The woman sat in her car, with the window half rolled down.

She looked at the reporter in wonder.

"I think you should probably take off that huge coat. It looks like you're sweating like crazy," she said.

"Indeed, but how would you explain the past few days weather wise? Have you ever seen anything like this?"

The woman took another long pause. She parsed her words in her head before she replied.

"Never, I'm just glad I'm on the right side of it."

The reporter, who had stripped himself of his cap and gloves, turned back to the camera. His eyes looked glazed over. The sweat had turned to a moist glisten that was pasted over his entire face. It created a reflection off the camera that made me squint.

"I'll tell you Sam, in all my years reporting I've never seen something this bizarre. Reporting live from the Salem/Middletown border, I'm John Casey. Back to you."

We were quiet as we waited for the news team in the studio to continue their coverage. They sat silent and provided no answers. Ten seconds of dead air. The three of them stared through the screen back at the three of us, silent as well.

The television went blank, dark for the next few minutes. Just long enough for mom to start to hyperventilate. She mumbled unanswerable questions to my dad, who sat in his recliner with an open can of beer.

"What are we going to do?" she asked.

"What can we do?"

"What if this never stops?"

"It has to," he said.

Dad's recliner squeaked as it took on his weight. He was thick enough in all the wrong places. His trusted seat, a mainstay in the home since I was a baby, had seen better days. It slanted to one side and even tipped over a few weeks back. It put dad right on his back.

The news returned with the anchor more confident and self-assured. His face had an added layer of makeup caked on. He tried to guide the news as best he could. He relayed the facts, kept away from speculation.

The camera cut to the weatherman who was standing in front of his map. Bobby told me recently that the map was a green wall in reality, that computer graphics added the map. He said that the weatherman's job was tough and thankless. He had to remember numbers and areas, where and when to point his finger.

The man started to explain that this thing was a once in a lifetime event. He pointed to a set of dark gray clouds that sat idle on the screen. They hovered over the middle of our town, aptly named Middletown. All systems, he explained, moved on. But he couldn't explain why these clouds, this thing, had stayed over us and chosen our town.

The freak appearance of the snow was lost in the initial shock of it all. As crazy as it was to have it in mid May, it was the way that it settled over only us that left everyone confused. No one, no matter what channel, had an answer. There was no mention of the fact that they hadn't predicted any snow. No analysis of how the weather mass went undetected on their expensive radar machines.

Dad grunted, swilled down the rest of his beer, and changed the channel. He said something about how these local idiots were in over their heads. He switched to the national news.

The last time I heard our town's name on a national channel was a few years ago while we watched a college football game. I never liked football, but dad did, so that's what we watched. It allowed him to play the part of dad, the best he knew how. He explained certain rules but mostly just pointed and yelled at the screen. He bombarded the television with theories of how each team could win. It gave him a purpose, a role. I played the part of dutiful son, hung on his every word, and nodded in agreement when prompted to. The kid from our high school was in the game, some huge school down south where football was religion. They showed a picture of him with the words "Hometown: Middletown" on the screen. My dad smiled, it silenced his anger for a moment. He was proud of someone he hadn't even known. The absurdity of the whole thing clashed against the seriousness in dad's eyes.

The national news anchor was calm and spoke with a loud voice. He was good at his job. He enunciated every syllable, took his time. He put our local news to shame as he reported the few known facts about the storm.

I had a second straight day off from school. Snow had blanketed the terrain, inched its way up off the ground, ankle deep in length. The accumulation started to corner our town off, isolated us from the rest of the world one flake at a time.

The sun was hidden. My eyes had adjusted to the darkness by now. We were stuck in a perpetual midnight. The town was sleepy except for the kids outside who played in their front yards. They dealt with the blizzard with their own creative acts. I was still stuck inside.

Most adults tore down the walls of snow, tried their hardest to push it aside. They acted like its appearance hadn't already intruded on their daily lives. Our family ignored it. Dad refused to give in to the snow. He figured it was only a matter of time before the sun would appear. He had some vacation time to burn. He wasn't going to spend his time out in the driveway, bundled up in May a foot deep in snow. Like everything else, it had turned into a contest, a personal duel. Him against nature. Mom and I knew who'd win, but we let him stand his ground for now. We didn't want to start another fight.

It took dad two weeks before he went outside to the garage to get the shovel. He did so with an attitude reserved for when my report card was littered with bad grades or when mom interrupted him in front of the television. He'd eaten up his two weeks paid vacation and had no more sick days until the start of next year.

I stayed inside and watched him from the window. He went out with a flannel shirt on, no coat. It was ten degrees outside with June just around the corner. He took small steps, wedged his feet outward like a penguin, and tried not to fall. Halfway there he did; right on his face. He remained there for a moment, frozen in place, as if he had given up, given in to the snow before he'd even began. A loud guttural scream came out from the deep of his belly. It echoed through the neighborhood, vibrated off our living room window.

He got to his feet and darted his head in my direction. I ducked down. He was embarrassed, didn't want witnesses to his folly.

The snow had grown heavy in the past few days. With the increased amount came the weight of each flake, like a complicated equation that added on to itself incrementally and steadily. He started at the end of the driveway and worked his way towards the house. Despite being mid afternoon, he almost snuck up on me as he reached the middle of the driveway. The fog had continued to force its way down towards us, amongst us. It reduced dad to nothing more than a shadowy figure that went in and out of visibility with each gust of wind. He tossed the shovel at the door of the garage, not able to turn its handle. He was drained, too tired to clear a path from the car to the house. He'd done half of the job and looked content with his progress.

He looked diminutive and fragile out there against the elements. I'd never seen him so vulnerable. He'd gone from a beast man trapped inside to a feeble old man stuck in the wilderness.

The local news reported that this was a town record for consecutive days off from school. The significance of the time off didn't hit me until we received the phone call. It was an automated message sent from the school. Mom stood at the kitchen doorway, phone line extended as far as it could go. She stared in my direction, over me and out the front window, to the darkness that had swallowed everything.

"That was your school. They said if this doesn't stop by next week that you'll have to come in during the summer to take your final exams," she said.

She was hiding now under multiple loosely fitted layers. Ratty old sweats that she used to wear when she called in sick to work.

I'd grown taller than her in the past year but it looked like she had shrunk. There were even a few strands of gray. I tried to place each strand to a specific event, something dad had done. Her eyes, the darkest shade of brown, were now lifeless. They'd become nothing more than a mirror to the outside weather we both watched all day long.

Underneath the layers was a tiny frame. She'd always been skinny, not like the cheerleaders or cross-country team at school but wiry, strung together like a more realistic version of Olive Oyl. I remembered a nightmare I had where dad was drunk and rolled over in bed and suffocated her to death.

"What? That's not fair, it's not like I'm on vacation. I'm stuck in the house all day!"

"They said that if you don't take your finals, if this weather doesn't stop before August, that everyone will be forced to repeat the year over."

The news had defeated me, silenced me. This thing had already eaten away at my life.

The promise, the allure of high school on the horizon next fall kept me going for much of that past winter. I imagined it as a place of possibilities, where my past didn't matter, where my future was infinite. Now there was nothing. No drastic makeover, nothing. Middle school, the smallness of it, was no longer an option. Something bigger was needed, a more expansive landscape to project my new personae on.

Dad came in, face bright red from the cold. His presence ripped me from my temporary fit. Sweat dripped from his forehead. He panted like that dog he promised me years ago. Snot hung frozen on the tip of his nose. His cheeks looked wind burnt like mine did the time when I fell asleep in my backyard fort made of snow a few years back.

Mom had found me under a pile of snow. She fed me chicken soup, made me drink cups of hot cocoa. Steam filled my nose as she tipped the mug upwards for me. I went to bed cold that night. Dad looked worse than that, like a monster.

"I gotta get going. I'll see y'all later." He looked at me, "Behave while I'm gone, you hear?"

"Where are you going?" Mom asked.

Mom had lost track of time. She'd been stuck at home with us. Her boss called her after the fourth straight day of snow and told her not to come in. He said it was temporary, that when things picked back up he'd call her. He told her not to worry.

It was weird to see mom out of her waitress uniform. I'd grown used to it as a sort of costume, like dad's flannels and boots. The only difference was that dad never changed his get up. Mom, without work, was naked. She looked uncomfortable even in her sweats. It was like she was lost. She just wandered around our home slowly, without any reason behind her moves. Without her job she was just another lonely housewife; a bored mom trapped inside all day.

"Work. Someone's gotta get some money."

"Thought you had some time," she said.

"It's all gone. Come morning I'll be back to regular schedule."

He grabbed his jacket and was out the front door before she could respond.

Now that dad was back at work it was just the two of us, all alone in the house. I remember when I was nine and had the chickenpox and mom stayed home with me all week. She fed me, read to me, and rubbed that stinky lotion all over me to help me not scratch.

The memory rushed back. I let it play out in my head as mom retreated upstairs to her bedroom for one of her naps. The darkness that rested beyond the walls outside vied for control.

That night four years ago was the last time we had spent quality time together. The years that followed had been full of busy schedules, double shifts, and homework. By the time I had reached some level of maturity, one step closer to being a man, I switched my allegiances. I latched on to my dad as if he could guide me the rest of the way into adulthood. He was even quieter with me than with mom. His main source of conversation was to complain about long hours at the factory, small paychecks, and a rotten past filled with regrets. My innocence frightened him, threatened his constructed exterior. My attempts with dad left mom abandoned, alone. She drifted through her monotonous days as she cleaned up after her two dependent boys.

As my need to scratch every itch subsided and the rashes disappeared, we played dress up. It was a Sunday night and the Oscars pre show had started. Dad was still at work, or at the bar. Mom put on her best dress, did herself up nice and good. Makeup, earrings, and necklace: the works. The few nice pieces of jewelry she had were family heirlooms, left to her in lieu of money or property. She yelled out for us to meet in her room in twenty minutes. "Be there or be square," she shouted as I dove into my closet and looked for my one nice suit. It was a gift from my mother's eccentric childhood friend who lived out in California.

Mom still had power over me back then, the ultimate allegiance of her only child. All she needed to do was give me that look. That exited look when her eyes would open up real wide and shimmer.

Full of confidence, and a smile as wide as in my parents wedding day photos, she looked beautiful, younger. That look had disappeared since, each successive day nothing more than a laundry list of real life problems that chipped away at her optimistic, youthful demeanor. Her eyes were bright with life, cheeks a rosy hue of playfulness. Her hair was done up in a fancy bun. She wore a long, black gown that looked brand new. Her jewelry sparkled. She was almost done with her make-up when she turned to look at me.

"Look at my handsome boy. You look marvelous. So grown up!"

She bent down and gave me a wet, sloppy kiss on my cheek.

"Mom, come on, that tickles. We're supposed to be playing. I'm a famous actor!"

She took a step back, tried her hardest to swallow her motherly instincts, and followed my lead.

"And who am I?"

"Well you're an equally famous actress. We just finished filming a popular movie where we were the leads. Everyone wants our autograph and everyone takes our picture, even when we go out to the store," I said.

"Uh-huh, well, shall we? The crowd is waiting for us downstairs. They're buzzing about, ready with their cameras and microphones, anxious for a piece of us."

I followed her lead down the steps. That night they were elegant, white marble steps draped with a red velvet carpet. The magical fabric hid our collective inadequacy as a family. I felt shaky and unsure of myself in this make-believe landscape. The dress shoes, which I'd worn once before, were stiff and tight. The formation of future blisters didn't stop me.

Halfway down she stopped and looked back up at me. The light overhead shone on her hair. She smiled in a way that I'd never seen before, or since, from her. The dress clung to her like she was a celebrity.

At the foot of the steps the real game began. We pretended that throngs of media were on either side, eager for their sound bites and photos. She clicked her tongue against the roof of her mouth to produce the clicks of the cameras. That was my cue to wave and smile. My head rotated as if on a swivel, as we made our way through the living room. On the television a man reported live from the actual red carpet. We followed his lead.

We stepped in the kitchen to give an exclusive interview. We couldn't afford to answer all the reporter's questions or we'd never make it inside in time. Mom lowered her voice, created a deeper, foreign sound. She played reporter first.

"So here we have Wilson Hart with us. Mr. Hart, it's a pleasure. First off, what are you wearing?"

She tried to stump me; her version of a pop quiz.

"It's so great to be here. I'm wearing a suit from a world famous Italian designer. He's blind in one eye and wears a patch. They call him the European Pirate. Very exclusive," I said.

She looked equal parts satisfied and proud of my on the spot imagination.

"Well you're up for a number of awards. Tell me, do you think you'll win?"

The question caught me off guard. I smiled and forced out a chuckle that turned to a childish cackle.

"Of course I want to win but there are so many great actors up for awards that there's no shame in losing. I'm just honored to be nominated."

"Mr. Hart thanks for your time and enjoy the night."

I nodded, played it cool as all the famous men in Hollywood did. We switched roles. Mom's answers weren't as creative, but she tried her best. After the questions she knelt down and said it was time for the big show and that we better get to our seats if we wanted to see the start of the awards. We didn't want to be rude to the hosts.

Mom waited for me outside the bathroom. She took me by the hand and brought me into the living room. On the couch were two pieces of paper with our names written on them.

We gave handshakes and hugs to the other members of our table. Mom introduced me to Brad Pitt and Angelina Jolie. He was handsome but had a messy beard. My clean-shaven face filled me with the confidence to give Angelina a wink.

Our television wasn't big, nothing compared to the one in Bobby's house, but it was large enough for that night. The deficiencies that surrounded us, the rips in the sofa, the holes in the carpet, the chipped paint on the walls, didn't matter anymore. They were still there of course; no amount of make-believe could erase our reality but that night gave us a temporary escape. I cuddled up close to mom on the couch and waited for the show to begin.

As the hosts appeared on stage mom turned off the lights and turned up the volume. It was like our own private movie theater. The presence of my return to school the next day didn't carry the same weight.

For the next three and a half hours we were important people. I didn't worry about homework, didn't care if dad stayed grumpy, didn't care if my parents continued to argue on a nightly basis. Nothing mattered because we were stars, famous and oblivious to the reality of the outside world. Neither of us won any awards. Mom heard me curse under my breath when they announced some French guy as the Best Actor. She smacked me on my thigh, still not out of her motherly role. Most of the jokes that the hosts told didn't make sense to me but I laughed when mom did. That was good enough because we shared something.

During one of the commercials Mom got up to make some popcorn. We ate it out of the fancy glass bowl that she reserved for holiday dinners. The butter stuck to my fingers and the salt clung to the sides of my throat. I filled up with soda, something usually banned at that time of night. The clock hit midnight, another step closer to school in the morning. Even though the show was almost done neither of us were ready to shed the clothes, the roles we had occupied.

As the final commercial break began the front door opened. A cold burst of wind blew into the house. Dad was drunk and shut the door slowly. His eyes gave it away every time, bloodshot and droopy. He looked like he hadn't slept in days. Behind the initial gust of cold night air came the stench of whiskey. At least that's what my mom always complained that he drank too much of. I remember she told him once that he loved whiskey more than her.

Mom's look of happiness had disappeared. The vibrancy in her cheeks evaporated, her eyes flushed of make-believe induced energy. She stared at the floor. We sat in silence as the show came back on. The host delivered his final punch line, the only one I understood all night, but dad's presence didn't allow me to laugh.

"What are you dressed up for? Y'all look like fucking idiots!"

And the award for best picture goes to…

"Answer me, god damnit!" he yelled.

"We were playing a game. Thought it'd be fun to play dress up for the Oscars. You know, to help Wilson get out his funk," she said.

"He's got chickenpox, not cancer!" He turned his gaze towards me, "Shouldn't you be in bed. If you're healthy enough to get dressed up and play like a girl than you're healthy enough for school."

Mom undid her hair and slipped off her earrings. She knew it was over. She'd given up, given in to dad's senseless reality.

I looked at mom, not sure what to say. It was best not to respond when dad was drunk. She looked over and nodded at me as if to say, save yourself. I jumped up from the couch and scurried past dad and up the stairs. He was hunched over and looked like he was up against an imaginary wall. He was tilted like the telephone pole out on the street that crept closer towards the ground each year.

I kept my door open to hear their argument. As long as dad wasn't in an aggressive mood his arguments were funny to listen to. The set of stairs protected me from his drunken tirade. It took every bit of imagination to convince myself that his screams were being directed at some strange woman, that they weren't insults towards mom.

I slept in my clothes that night.

The next few weeks I was a prisoner in my own house. Jailed by the storm and suffocated by the darkness. Mom stayed home with me. She didn't have much say in the matter. She knew her boss wasn't going to call her. Things had gotten worse. The local news ran updates on the thing every twenty minutes. The clouds hadn't moved an inch in four weeks. Nothing, not even a single ray of sunshine peeked through the dark mass that hovered above us.

Word had it that the neighboring town had set up a refuge of sorts. They cleared the hotel for families that needed to leave the storm. They offered rooms at half price but that was still too expensive for dad. He wasn't going to admit defeat, and he wasn't going to pay to admit that. I knew this handout wouldn't apply to us.

I hadn't seen Bobby since school closed. When the local news first reported that this thing might go on indefinitely. I assumed Bobby and his family would take off for safer ground.

He stopped by to say goodbye before he left. His dad beeped the car horn from the curb, impatient with the intensity of the storm. He was vague about their plans, said something about going to his grandparents' house upstate. He shook my hand and nodded. There was no need to ask about my plans. He knew that my dad was going to stay put. He wished me well and skipped down the icy steps and into the snow pile. I wanted to go with him, but their car was already full of their own memories. There was no room for me.

My best friend had left, gotten out before it got worse. We weren't as lucky, didn't have enough saved to do the same. Dad's stubbornness wouldn't allow us to head for safer ground.

Dad worked as many hours as he could at the factory. He realized the seriousness of our situation, our town's collective condition, but was powerless. We all were. Soon he was at the factory sixteen hours a day, double shifts, six days a week. It was how he dealt with the chaos around us. How he kept his mind off of our bleak situation.

On Sundays he sat motionless in the living room, eyes glued to the television screen. His hands were gripped around a can of beer and a lit cigarette. We both knew to leave him alone, let him fester among his thoughts. He wallowed, produced grunts and belches or loud sighs every so often that coincided with the news updates. Despite the entire news team being focused on the storm they didn't find anything in it. Even the sports reporter tracked the storm. The harder they looked the less they seemed to find.

Now even national news outlets began to descend upon our town. They announced their arrival with large vans and elaborate satellites on top. They rolled in a dozen deep. They antagonized our small town with their presence, as if we had missed something important, some vital piece of information that would fill out the picture. They headed to the news station first to mark their arrival like dogs. Within a few hours they had spanned out throughout the town. They crept block by block like zombies in search of the living.

One van stopped on our street and parked a few houses down from us. A large crew jumped out, opened the back of the van, and fetched their equipment. Yards of cords were untangled, cameras were readied, microphones doled out, earpieces hooked up, and lights fanned out in the background to illuminate the correspondent. She was much prettier than any of our reporters. From a distance she resembled a Barbie doll. Her bleached blonde hair shone through the darkness. I stayed at the window in anticipation of their next move. They looked the part, competent and efficient. If anyone could solve our conundrum, diagnose this thing, it was them. It had to be, we couldn't do it ourselves.

Dad's truck turned the corner. It lost traction for a moment as it went over the solid ice sheet that covered the pavement. He slowed down at the sight of the van and lowered his window as he approached them. He stayed there, stopped in the middle of the road for a minute before he continued to our driveway.

Dad jumped out from the driver's seat and fell into the snow that reached up to his crotch. From my vantage point our front yard looked like a bunch of whack-a-mole holes. Dad struggled through the snow like a robot, his legs mechanical in their movements, as if they were both attached to well-worn pogo sticks. The situation that dad, this grown-up mammoth, found himself in was comical. He made it to the front door, his jeans soaked, boots covered in white powder and frozen solid. I ran to the bottom of the stairs as he opened the door.

"What'd you say to them out there?"

"What?"

He looked confused, out of breath.

"To the reporters. Did you say anything when you stopped?" I asked.

"No."

"But you rolled your window down."

"Just wanted a better look at the blonde. She's got the nicest rack I've ever seen in person."

He brushed by me and stomped into the kitchen, didn't give me a chance to respond. She did look like she belonged on television.

Even from a distance her beauty looked fake. Too perfect for this type of place, to be among us townies.

That night we ate dinner in silence. As the news stations surrounded us we closed ranks and retreated within the four walls that surrounded our lives.

My days had morphed into one long, continuous event. There were still moments of levity but they were forced. There was nothing to be happy about and we all knew it. As the clouds and darkness lingered, mom's mood took a turn for the worse. Seasonal depression came up on my Internet search. The description was technical and removed. Part of me wished it were more than the weather that troubled her. She deserved more than this. There was no way that she could be content if only this weather stopped. Could she? Had her expectations of happiness dropped so low? Had life sucked out all the joy? Both of us had taken a piece from her, chipped away each day to the point that her life was work, clean, cook and repeat. This thing reinforced what I'd tried to avoid all these years. It forced me to watch mom's slow demise. I wished there was something that could be done, some way to show her that she wasn't alone. But there wasn't, her life was different from mine. Sacrifice ruled her world.

Dad internalized his feelings. He was able to get out of the house and go to work. As the snowfall strengthened, he drank more. Each drink he finished, each belch he let out, reminded me of the dad that he wasn't. The one that never played catch with me. It was irrelevant that we didn't have a big enough yard. It was the thought, or lack thereof, that mattered most to me, and least to him.

School called later that week. It was the first phone call in days. I scampered down the stairs, eager to hear a different voice. Mom gave me the same look that she had the last time the school called. It was an automated message but she reacted as if she were annoyed at a living person. Her complaints and frustrations were all she had left. Her half-hearted attempts at disgust thrown in every direction were looked at with the same contempt by dad as my temper tantrums.

School had been cancelled. The remaining semester, final exams and all, were postponed indefinitely.

Dad's reaction to the news was proactive in a way that caught me off guard. After dinner he mumbled out the idea that I could help out down at the factory. He tried to sneak it in while mom was wrist deep in soapy dishwater.

"No way is my baby working at that place," she said.

She emphasized the word to make her judgments clear and known to dad. He took offense to her statement. He usually did.

"What's that supposed to mean?"

"It's not the type of place, it's not the type of work that he should be doing. He should stay here, at home, and continue his studies independently. Besides, he can help me around the house."

Dad let out a chuckle. He rubbed his belly and pushed his chair away from the table.

"So, what, that's it? You're answer is to turn him into mommy's little helper? What a joke."

"Make fun of it all you like but I'm not letting you take him down to the factory," she said.

"Why not?"

"It's not where he belongs."

"Some hard work never hurt no one. You think he's too good to get a little a dirty?"

Dad asked questions when they fought that they both already had the answers to. It was his way of undermining her thoughts.

"He's too smart for that place. All it's done to you is make you sit around and reminisce about your glory days. You're not gonna suck him into that."

"What the fuck are you talking about glory days? Trust me, ain't nothing glorious about my past. It'll be temporary and we need the extra money since you're not working."

"This isn't about me not working!"

He had done it again. She stopped and gathered her thoughts. She didn't want to play into his point that she was too emotional, not in charge.

"You said it would be temporary when you started. Remember that? You promised that when Wilson grew up a little, you'd go back and finish your G.E.D. You even promised to get a certificate from the community college so you could go back and run the plant, not just stand at the assembly line. Look how well that worked out! He's not going to the plant. Period."

She got out of her chair and headed for the living room, out of breath from her monologue, cheeks flushed with years of pent-up rage. Dad sat with me in the kitchen, silent. He'd never seen her fight back like that, stand her ground. I hadn't either. All of their fights were one-sided. She made me proud, honored that she had stood up for me, and herself. Maybe this weather, this thing, would produce something good after all.

Everyone went to bed quietly that night. There was nothing to talk about and no more arguments to be won. Dad slept on the couch, still in his work clothes. The sound of a large crack followed by a dull thud woke me up early, startled me. Outside our house a large tree had snapped right at the base under the weight of all the snow. It fell forward and cut the power lines that ran down our street on impact.

Sparks from the lines exploded like Fourth of July fireworks on the icy sidewalk. They fizzled out fast as the snow covered up the black lines in less than a minute.

The clock next to dad's recliner blinked the same number and none of the lights worked. We'd lost power. All the news reports warned us about power outages if the storm continued. Dad had shrugged off the idea as propaganda to get us all riled up. Another way for the media to make us rush out and pick up extra supplies. His conviction, his certainties, about his opinions were enough to reel me in, enough make me believe him.

He woke up as I stood over him in silence.

"What?" he mumbled.

"Power's out. Guess the news was right."

"It's probably nothing. Won't last more than two days guaranteed."

He got up, stretched his arms out like a giant bear and gulped down the rest of the warm can of beer from the table beside him.

"Tell your mom I'll be home late. Gonna get into work early, make sure the outage is only local."

I nodded and watched him as he stumbled out of the house still half asleep. Dad struggled to get his truck out of the driveway. He finally got his tires on the ground and slid right up over the sidewalk, over the damaged power lines, and out onto the street. His tires had kicked up the lines, gave them new life, rid them of their snow-covered hideout and brought them out into the open once again. As he turned and went down the street, the phantom sounds of the power lines still hummed in my ear.

I sat in total darkness for the rest of the day. The occasional car, with their hazards on, provided a brief shimmer of light. The yellowish white tints from the headlights were hard to make out through the darkness. I could hear them before they appeared on the street. They invaded my space, forced themselves into my living room as they turned onto my street and flashed through the windows. Even at such slow speeds the passengers were invisible. Our street looked like a part of those elaborate mechanical train sets that the rich kids got for Christmas.

By lunchtime, a local crew had come out to work on the broken power line. They remained parked for an hour. I reached for my binoculars to get a better look. Since the darkness, they were always nearby. They were my access to the outside world.

Both men were fat, middle-aged, and bundled up in layers of clothes. They sat, busy with their lunch. Foot longs of piled deli meats shoved into their mouths with a slow, steady precision that if applied to the scene feet from their van, would clear the mess produced by this thing in no time. They both had multiple chins, mayonnaise plastered on their content faces.

A plow came through. It was the third that morning. Every few feet it would hit a patch of ice and lose its traction. The plow skidded across the street and forced the driver to hit the brakes, back up, and retrace his steps. The process was slow, unproductive at best. At the sound of the machine, the men in the van put away their food and fell into the pile of snow that had accumulated on the side of the street.

It took them five minutes to reach the back of the van. They trudged through the damp, heavy snow with grimaces on their faces. They took out orange cones. The reflectors provided a glimmer of light. They started to dig out the white piles in search of the power line. They were in a rush against the elements, scared to freeze. As the snowfall increased, the men disappeared entirely. Now it fell at the rate of three or four inches per hour. I layered up and made my way onto the front porch, flashlight in hand, to get a better look. Boredom had turned me into one of those easily annoyed neighbors; like an old man with nothing better to do than stick his nose in everyone else's business.

The men didn't notice my presence. My light wasn't on them directly, instead I focused it on the area that they had dug out. They reached the wire and looked at one another to see whose turn it was to work. The fatter of the two lost the battle and bent over and stuck his gloved hands into the snow. He came up with the broken off end of the wire. Its life had long since been frozen over by the weather. He started to grab at it like a rope in a game of tug of war. They both inched their way, one after the other, to the split in half pole further down the road. When they got to the pole, the fatter of the two took out a knife and chopped at the root of the line in a hurry. He gathered the wire, now free from the pole, and threw it towards the van. Then he refocused his energy on the pole.

The other guy had gone back to fetch more tools. The sound of a chain-saw being revved up clashed with the sound of the plow as it came down the street. The man plodded through the snow bank on the sidewalk, power tool in front of him. It lead the way as it ripped through the cold dark air. He reached the pole and finished what the weather had started. He broke off the top of the pole from the base and then went to work on the bottom. Once the saw penetrated the frozen exterior it churned through the rotten wood in a matter of seconds, left only a stump.

The plow had reached our house. It had gained momentum, thrown the snow to the side without a care. A pile hit both of them, threw them to the ground. One man jumped to his feet and began to yell at the plow driver. I shone the light on where the other worker had fallen. He still had yet to emerge from the white pile. The one on his feet turned at once and yelled out to me but it was muffled. As he pawed through the snow, on all fours, like a dog in search of a buried bone, he looked up and yelled again, this time louder and more clearly.

"Get some fucking help!"

I rushed down the few stairs that led up to our door, slipped on the final one from a coat of ice that had formed and fell over. From this angle the snow in the front yard looked like a huge fluffy pillow. Halfway there the blood became visible. My flashlight had distorted the color slightly; made it look bolder, like a bottle of ketchup had exploded.

The drop from the front yard down off the curb and onto the street caught me, tripped me up, forced me to scramble the rest of the way on all fours out to the base of the power line.

"Shit, shit, shit. What the fuck just happened?"

The man talked to no one in particular. He shook his head. Disbelief and the weather had overcome him.

I felt something with my hands and dropped the flashlight into the snow. It felt like a stick. It was a detached arm, from the elbow down, bloody, hard, and cold. Just in front of me the rest of the body came into focus. My flashlight had illuminated everything. The man was face up, eyes open, unblinking. His head was split open, a huge gash about the size of the stump of what was left from the pole. The pole had blood and hair and skin on it. The flakes did their best to cover it, as if it never happened. My stomach flipped and began to move north towards my throat. The soup, from earlier, came out of me in one long spray. Chunks of chicken now caked on top of the dead workers torso.

Mind racing and body numb, I chased after the plow. I needed to get away from the blood, the disaster, in my front yard. I got to the plow before it turned onto a new street and pelted it with snowballs. The driver stopped the engine, took off his headphones, and jumped out of the truck in one swift motion. He came at me fast and had a mean look on his face. He stopped as he neared me, eyes focused on the blood on my jacket and hands.

"What the hell happened to you?"

"We...you need to call for an ambulance."

"I'll get on with my radio dispatcher back at the village building. What happened? Are you alright?"

"You, you killed a man back there down the road," I said.

"What? How? What are you talking about?"

I took a deep breath. A lungful of cold air rushed through me and hit the back of my chest, centered me as my mind fumbled around for the right words.

"Back there, down the road, you threw up a pile of snow where those guys were working. One guy, he fell onto his chainsaw. Cut his arm right off. Huge gash right through his head. He's dead."

The driver looked away from me, focused his eyes on the snowflakes. He started to cry to himself.

When we got there the body hadn't moved and the other worker turned and looked at us, eyes darkened like a rabid raccoon. Blood was everywhere. My front yard had become a pool of another man's demise.

We kept our distance from the body and the worker. Me out of respect, the driver out of fear. He'd already done enough, caused this whole incident. I watched, frozen, as the other worker tried to resuscitate his friend's limp body.

It took the ambulance a half hour to arrive. My sense of time, surrounded by this mangled body, had reappeared. All of my senses were heightened.

Mom appeared at the doorstep, still in her nightgown. She must've heard the sounds of the ambulance, which skidded to a hectic stop inches from the van's back bumper. As I approached the steps her face slowly came into focus. I felt like a child who had run home from a playground accident. This time she couldn't kiss the pain away. No Band-Aids or rubbing alcohol would diminish this sting.

She noticed the blood on my hands and began to check me from head to toe. Her dark brown eyes couldn't hide her fear. I hadn't received this type of attention in years.

"Are you okay?"

"Fine."

I sounded like my dad.

"What happened? Who is that out there?"

She looked over my shoulder, out into the wintery dark.

"A worker, he died," I said.

"Oh my God! Did you see it?"

I shook my head. No words could do justice to what had just happened. Mom sprang forward, arms outstretched as she enveloped me in her bosom. She tried to hug away the shock still visible in my eyes.

The cops were close behind. They had to get in between the worker and the driver who started to have a go at it. Each man was put into separate cars. The officers returned from their patrol cars ready with their clipboards and reports to fill out. To put on record that they'd done their job, completed what was asked of them. The blood on my hands had dried and turned a syrupy color as they asked me questions with the emotion of a doctor. Words like incident replaced death. They blunted the trauma with a formality that fueled my own lack of emotions. I told them what I knew, which wasn't much and what I saw, which was too much. They offered me their card, the words typed neatly on it obscured by snowflakes by the time it was in my hand.

Dad came home early that night. He was quiet as he entered. Sober with his footsteps as he made his way towards the back of the house. I remained in the kitchen since the cops left. There were still splatters of blood strewn about the sidewalk, which led up to our door. Mom sat across the table with her cup of tea in silence. She bobbed the packet up and down, in and out of the cold cup of water. She didn't know what to say, had no words to fill the empty room, to remove the seen, to make me forget.

"Man it's a ghost town out there, no one on the road. The plant was half full; in fact..." he looked up, interrupted by our silence. "What the hell happened here?"

He looked me over. There was a layer of dried blood caked on. It looked like one of those Jackson Pollock paintings that my art teacher had us study.

Mom got up, headed towards the sink. She began to run the water. She wanted to hear a noise, some subtle background to fill the emptiness that threatened to swallow us whole.

"Well?

"There was an accident," she said.

"I'm asking him," he said.

I sat there, unmoved by his last comment. He pressed further.

"What the fuck is goin' on here? Whose blood is that Wilson?"

More silence. Dad's eyes said it all, full of tiredness from a day of brutal grunt work on his feet. There was enough pain behind them already. There wasn't any need to add more weight on his shoulders.

"Wilson, answer me for fuck's sake!"

"Leave him be honey. He's been through a lot," she said.

She faced him now. She'd thrown me a life raft, an escape route. I took it without a second thought.

"What the hell are y'all talking about? What happened?"

I rushed past them and went upstairs, hurried by the need to scrub myself clean, rid myself of the afternoon's horror.

"Hey, I'm not finished with you!" he yelled.

Their voices grew muffled with each step towards the second floor. I couldn't listen to mom struggle to put into words what I'd been through. I ran the water for a bath, couldn't fathom a shower, my knees were too weak. My whole body was tired from the afternoon's cold air. It had stung me, pierced through my clothes and flesh, went straight for the bones. My knees and ankles ached, barked out in pain.

The stream of ice-cold water forced me to refocus my thoughts. The water's temperature held supremacy, the power to eliminate its surroundings, to make them unnecessary, irrelevant. There was no need to dip myself into the tub. I stopped the water as it reached the brim and slipped in, one motion, no hesitation. The cold water enveloped me. My extremities went numb. I had become less than the sum of my parts, was incomplete now, physically broken to match my mindset.

The blood had dried up, become a part of me. It had seeped into my pores, pushed to get deeper inside. A wash towel wouldn't suffice; this needed bare hands. My fingers ran against my wet arms slowly as the remains of the worker rubbed off me. I'd taken control of the situation, repossessed what was momentarily taken from me a few hours earlier.

The blood mixed with the clear water around me. It started to congeal in the water, like an oil spill in the ocean. As the water turned light red, the waves of the blood circled out further to reach the boundaries of the tub. I twirled my fingers through the water and picked up handfuls to examine the death in my palms. It swam through my fingers and back into the pool. Much like the experience, the memory of the event, it couldn't be contained.

The man's presence was all around me. The tub was plugged so the blood wouldn't drain away. This was the last of him, the last chance to physically deal with what had happened. The rest of his remains would be pieced back together like some puzzle, packed into a closed coffin. My body now returned to its normal pale hue. I bent forward, opened my mouth and took a gulp of water. Swished it around my mouth for a moment, like mouthwash, before it went down. It had happened so fast that something had to be taken with me, to keep inside of me for a few more days.

After weeks of boredom, this event happened and had turned my life upside down. It forced me into the present, collided with this thing, this weather, with my own enclosed life. It became crystal clear, in that moment, that this thing wasn't going anywhere soon. It had bigger plans for us regardless of what we did. The darkness had infected our town, hovered over us. It was no longer content with power outages and snowfall totals. It wanted blood; it was out for the taste of human flesh. The sound of hail as it clinked against the window, convinced me that this thing had a soul, and wanted us to conform to it. Every drop of snow it produced was like a heartbeat, a reminder that it was there and ready to pounce.

My parent's yells were audible through the thin walls and old floorboards. They echoed through our dilapidated house. Deep breaths, clear mind, I went under. Completely submerged, I pushed myself to the limit, wanted to see how much pain my body could endure. Muffled and wavy at the corners, my vision became strained. My eyes started to burn. I forced them to remain open, fearful to blink, scared that I'd lose the power of the moment. My nostrils began to flare, anxious for air. Bubbles of silent desperation sprang to the surface.

Stillness was the goal, a need to become the moment rather than a part of it. It had consumed me, taken me in its harsh arms and cradled me to sleep. I could've given up right there. The thoughts had been there for a while. Ideas of what death would feel like, what the afterlife would taste and smell like had haunted me before but this was different. Now I had moved towards it.

At the three-minute mark, my head raised up from the water slowly, as to show that the idea of death didn't scare me. Beads of water clung to my skin as the cold air of the room blanketed my chilled body with its big embrace.

The house had gone silent. The lone noise came from outside. The thing had picked up strength, only somewhat satiated from its earlier conquest. It wanted more, it wanted to inflict more damage, impose its will on us. The prospects for the future seemed bleak.

The conversation stopped when I entered the kitchen. Both of them looked through me. Dad had a glass of water. Alcohol wasn't necessary. Mom no doubt filled him in on what had happened. He shared our recognition of the seriousness of the moment. His eyes, no longer slow and droopy, darted around the room. He was sober, and terrified.

The food on the table had grown cold. I joined them at the table in silence, waited for someone to break through the wall of quiet and fear with words, no matter how trivial. Dad was deep in thought, inverted.

He became more withdrawn each moment. He fell further into his own thoughts.

"The plant is closed as of midnight. Boss didn't even have the balls to tell us himself. He just posted a note on the board by our time cards."

Dad's words reverberated, sent out shockwaves to the rest of us. Mom sat stunned in submission.

"What are we gonna do for money?" I said.

Mom looked to dad. She pleaded with her eyes for him to field my questions, to ease my worries.

"We'll figure it out. Don't you worry about it. You keep up with your studies. Just because school is canceled doesn't mean you can sit around all day doing nothing," he said.

He looked at mom to see if he had handled it correctly. She looked surprised, relieved that he had backed off his previous statements of me going to work. These weren't his words; they were lines from mom's script. She'd stood up for me. His grip on the emotional atmosphere of the house was loosened, but things were different now. The man's death had forever changed me, hardened me so that I started to build up my defenses against my surroundings just as my parents had softened towards me. Dad's empathy was foreign to me; his harshness was temporarily gone.

We finished our meal. There was a calmness, an order to the whole thing. It felt like those times when mom used to force us to go to Church and listen to the Father's words. I always suspected that she used God to punish the two men in her life. Put us back into the roles that she had predetermined for us.

Mom left the table and gave me a kiss on the forehead. The plates were still on the table, dirtied from a half eaten dinner. She recognized the severity of the situation, knew the importance of us being alone. She had allowed dad some wiggle room in their plan of how to deal with me. They'd come to an agreement, had ended their argument in unison for once.

It was our first real moment together in years. Dad's effort, his willingness to sit and talk rather than slam a door in response to an event, was significant.

"Alright, enough bullshit. What happened? Don't go holding back on me either."

Before he finished his sentence he opened the pantry, his words lost as his back faced me. He reappeared with a bottle of whiskey in one hand and two glasses in the other. He went into the living room, me a few steps behind him. He waited for me to start. I sat, silent, ready to wait him out, curious about the second glass.

He poured himself a full glass, the other a third of the way. He passed it along the table. The sound of the bottom of the glass against the grain of the wood was amplified against our silent glares. He pulled out two cigarettes, placed each in his mouth and lit them with his Zippo. A flick of the wrist that showcased his unique talent. Without an exhale he unlipped one cigarette, turned it around so the flame faced him and reached across the table. I took it, careful not to drop it, without any idea as to how to proceed. My every move felt magnified, under his microscopic lens. He sat back in his recliner, hands full with his two vices, and shot me a foreign look. He no longer looked through me. For this moment were equals. I had a story to tell, an experience to share, and he wanted to soak in every word.

"It ain't gonna smoke itself."

Despite the half finished packs strewn about the house over the years this was my first cigarette. I used to place them in my mouth and talk into the mirror. Pretended to be John Wayne, Clint Eastwood, wanted my words to guide the end of the cigarette, to use it as a weapon. Imagined that it had the power to keep my make believe audience at a distance. The cigarette rested in my hand, unsmoked. The three-inch crooked line of ash broke up on its way to the floor as it glanced off my arm. I took it to my lips, sucked in hard, and waited. My mouth began to feel like the embers of a campfire log. A plume of smoke escaped from my mouth. Dad's laughter broke the cloud up as it reached him.

"Do it again. This time after you suck in go for another breath. Open up your lungs and take a deep breath before you exhale."

I did as commanded, not quite his equal after all. But his tone was different, his body language more relaxed. He acted like he did when he'd come home from the bar and take mom upstairs. Played it cool and nonchalant. My stream of thought was broken up when the smoke hit my lungs. It pierced holes in my chest, dared me to cough up everything inside. I wanted to hold out, to act the part, but was unable to. A mouthful of throw up dripped from my mouth like when mom used to feed me liquid vegetables in my high chair. There were some kids in my grade at school who'd attempted to smoke in front of me. They needed a crowd to witness the event. Like it would legitimize their attempt as they strained to grasp some semblance of manhood that they'd heard about.

There was no laughter at the other end of the room. Not this time. He'd observed my attempt at manliness and even though it resulted in abject failure, he held his sarcastic remarks for another time. This night leveled the playing field; I'd gained on him. Tipped the scales a notch towards the middle.

"Drink some, it'll wash away the taste in your mouth," he said.

I sipped from the glass. He abandoned his usual gulps in favor of my hesitant pinch of whiskey. It wasn't the taste that slowed me. The smell, fire tinged acid, struck my nostrils with a ferocity that had only been matched by the odor of death from earlier.

"Now, what'd you see?"

He leaned in, as if to accentuate the question mark. This was new for me. Never saw him like this, so curious, so empty and in need of something to fill him up.

"A man died."

This wouldn't satisfy him but I wanted to see how far, how explicit, the story would have to get.

"No shit," he said.

He was on his second cigarette and had already poured a second glassful of whiskey. He picked up his pace, like he was with his buddies down at the bar. He left the bottle and pack of smokes in the middle of the table, gave me silent permission to indulge.

"It happened so fast yet it seemed like it went by in slow motion. Does that make sense?"

"Not really."

"It was like a movie that wasn't quite cued up properly. But then, when it was over everything came to a stop. It slowed down to a crawl. Like the events of what happened was forcing me to replay everything over and over," I said.

"You know your granddad said something like that after he came back from the war. Not right away. He was quiet for a long, long time, but eventually he spoke about what he saw. First time my old man ever treated me like a man, and this was after I'd married your mom and she was pregnant with you."

"So, you're treating me like a man now too?"

I regretted the question. Wished there were a way to take it back, afraid that the moment was somehow tarnished. My immaturity was exposed by a need to put words to what we were doing. Dad sat back in his chair, less serious now.

"Have some more whiskey," he said.

"Why? Does it solve anything?"

"Learned a long time ago that booze may not be the answer but it sure does make you forget the question."

With each tick of the clock the realization that this night, this moment shared, was almost over made me anxious. Pressed for time, the confessions of what happened came out that much easier. It was a race against time. I didn't know if he'd ever be interested in one of my stories ever again.

Lightheaded and loose from the liquor, I overindulged. Basked in the temporary attention that dad bestowed upon me. His glare increased the tension between us as the horrors of what took place left my mouth. Even with half a bottle of whiskey in him and his movements slow and more deliberate, his look punctured me. It stung my extremities like a hornet and rested somewhere in my chest, right next to the liquor.

"You know, I've seen my fair share of fucked up shit," he said. "When

I first started working at the factory a guy on the assembly line got his sleeve caught in the roller. Man, did he bleed. His hand got taken clean off. Never thought I'd last the month." He stopped, to find the point of his story. "Anyway, just had to tell myself that those type of things happen everyday you know?"

"But what does it mean? How did you get over it?"

He tossed a cigarette into my lap, lit his and flung the lighter towards me. He exhaled through his nose, a favorite move of his. He leaned forward again, now reengaged in the conversation.

"Stuff like that happens everyday and that I'm lucky it wasn't me. The biggest lesson you'll ever learn is that most of the time in life you have no control," he said.

I looked outside for confirmation. His words rang true as the snow continued.

"Once you stop fighting that and accept it and move on you'll be better off."

His thoughts trailed off, a side effect of the whiskey infused therapy session he'd practiced since he was my age.

"That's easier said than done, no?"

"Never said nothing about it being easy, just said it was necessary. Big difference," he said.

He began to doze off. The lit cigarette inched closer to his fingertips. It looked tiny in his huge paw of a hand. Even though I'd seen him drunk countless times, we never had the chance to hang out while he was drunk. He was usually busy with mom. It was either an apology or an argument. It felt good to gain this access to him, to know that mom didn't have complete ownership of his intoxicated moments.

"It may not make sense now," he said, as he bolted to an upright position, fingers darkened from the tip of his cigarette. He looked down as if shocked by the cigarette's appearance, like it was some prop a stranger had placed in his hand. "But someday, when you're older, it will."

He drained what was left in his glass, stubbed out his smoke, and got up from his chair. He navigated his way around the coffee table in my direction. Through the smoke and my whiskey filled eyes my body tensed up for a moment, prepared for the unknown, the indefensible. His frame blacked out the candles, minimized everything in the background. I had no idea what he was going to do next. His breath was heavy as it fell down on my face. He put a hand on my shoulder, bent down, and kissed me on my forehead.

"Have a goodnight."

I didn't respond. Couldn't find the words to say thank you, to commemorate the significance of the moment. I watched him ascend the staircase. He took each step as a mini hurdle, his every move deliberate and off pace.

The snow had turned to hail. Individual white pellets beat down on our house as if shot from a b.b. gun. Sleep wouldn't come easy that night. I was wide awake from the day's events despite the alcohol. My dad's boots made their way to the bed in the middle of the room upstairs before the house fell silent.

A few candles remained lit for the rest of the night. They refused to fade out, as if they knew about our situation and had decided to stay vigilant. Outside only the weather was awake, like practice for the daytime. I filled my glass, grabbed a cigarette, and began to smoke purposefully. Allowed my lungs to become filled with toxins in an effort to match my feelings.

I had, in a small way, become my dad. That's what the night had been all about. It was a way to prove myself. My dad let his guard down. He now appreciated me more because of what I'd been through. We now shared a common bond. This event, this hardship that was in its infancy within me, was something he could relate to. He had me beat, no doubt a lifetime of struggles under his belt already. I had notched a tally, been a part of life's cruel plans, imagined that the day's events could've figured as prominently as the dartboard and jukebox in the bar that dad bellied up to nightly.

Most boys grew closer to their dad's through sports or cars. We had tragedy and disappointment to relate with. The proximity to death was my chance at a relationship with him.

With the bottle emptied and the ashtray filled, I'd gained confidence. My maturity felt like a tangible thing now. This ownership kept me wired. It elevated me above visions of that worker's death into a realm of boldness that was missed by not being the coolest or most athletic guy in my grade.

I turned the television on in the hopes of something. There was nothing, still scrambled flakes of black and white that matched the scenery outside. The local news station had long ago stopped their display of the daily sunrise and sunset times. They had resigned themselves to this thing. Now with the power off we had shared in what had become the new normal.

Dad came downstairs before my mom.

"Quick, we gotta clean this up before your mom sees this. She'll cut my balls off if she knew you were drinking and smoking."

Dad handed me some breath mints. Mom began to prepare breakfast before she realized that she could offer nothing more than dry cereal and tepid water. As she let out an exasperated grunt dad chuckled and gave me a wink.

Mom called us together for a family meeting. Last time she did that was when she walked in on me as I masturbated for the first time. Dad laughed the whole time, mumbled something about boys being boys. Mom held her tears back as she scolded me.

This time it wasn't my fault. In a way, death and this thing had gotten me off the hook. My actions were hidden within the darkness and confusion.

"Maybe it wouldn't be such a bad thing if we went over and stayed with Jeff and Marcy for a while. Nothing permanent, just until this storm ends," she said.

Dad turned to me and rolled his eyes. Marcy was mom's sister. She lived about two hours away in a nice area. Dad would crack on mom when he got drunk, asked if they came from the same family. She never laughed.

Marcy was a lawyer and Jeff was a dentist. They had a lot more money than us. It was weird that they lived in a huge house but didn't have any kids. Not even a pet. Just four empty, spare bedrooms that were decorated from a page out of those expensive design store magazines.

The last time we visited them was a year ago. We stayed for a week. It was mom's idea. Something bad happened during Marcy's pregnancy and now we needed to show our love and support. Those were mom's words. She spoke to Aunt Marcy in hushed tones while dad was forced to watch golf and drink expensive domestic light beer with Jeff. Uncle Jeff would rub my head and call me champ.

"No," dad said.

"I'm thinking out loud. What do you propose we do, stay in the house with no heat or electricity for God knows how long?"

Dad let out a sigh for show. He looked to me and hoped for some back-up, something that would get us out of this visit.

"Come on, what about me? I hate that place. The house is like a museum. I'm scared that I'll break one of their precious sculptures. Besides Uncle Jeff treats me like a little kid and Aunt Marcy hates me!"

Dad held back his smile. He was satisfied that I'd at least prolonged the situation. He hated to play dress up, especially for people he didn't like. His unworn polo shirts and khakis collected dust in the back of his closet for a reason.

"Don't say that honey. Of course your Aunt Marcy loves you. Ever since she lost her baby she's been a bit emotional and seeing you I'm sure reminds her of what she doesn't have."

"Whatever, it's still creepy that she doesn't talk to me. She just sits and stares at me like she does," I said.

"Look, I'm not going to sit here in a cold, dark house indefinitely," mom said.

We'd have to meet her halfway, make some compromise in order to stay put.

"Alright, enough. Don't get all emotional. I'll go out and get a few space heaters, generators, more batteries, flashlights, and candles. The works, okay? We're not gonna get up and abandon our home because of a storm," dad said.

Dad left the kitchen with the word storm still fresh on his tongue. He slammed the front door shut. A pile of snow drifted inside, a reminder of what waited for us outside.

The house was frigid and dark. A harsh cold that ripped through the flesh and attacked the bones. A few more days like this and there'd be little difference between outside and inside. No more sanctuary, no protection from the elements.

Mom hated the cold. She internalized its unfriendliness and regurgitated it back on dad. She sulked in the darkness of our home. She let the shadows overcome her, replaced her usual apathetic demeanor with something more hostile. It brought out the worst in her. She was ill equipped for the cold weather and had begun to wilt under the pressures of her surroundings.

After dad left I found her upstairs in her closet. She thumbed through dozens of garage sale sundresses. She was in mourning, dealt with the loss of summer in her own way. The closet was dark but she pawed through it as if she knew the location of every piece.

Her hands discerned each article by their texture. She stopped as she heard me in the doorway. She stood frozen, like she'd lost in a game of hide and seek.

"You okay?" I asked.

"Yeah just wish these dresses could get some use soon. I've been looking forward to summer all year. It's so liberating, you know? The nice weather allows us to be whoever we want to be, like play time as a child. The sun is the audience in a grand game of make believe."

Mom was always a bit eccentric. It was her response, her way to deal with her domestication. Every so often her true nature would come out. The wild, free spirited young woman who was ready to experience life.

"Well my vacation has turned into a fucked up weather event. Like some footnote that scientists will be talking about when I'm older," I said.

"Hey, what'd I tell you about using that kind of language?"

"Sorry, it's just that I'm bored…and mad."

"Well that's no excuse for speaking like that. God, you're starting to sound like your father."

"Is that such a bad thing?"

"You're smarter than that. There's no need to hide your intelligence behind guttural language," she said.

Certain lines had been drawn, opposite ends taken, in our household. Mom saw in me infinite potential. I was a lump of clay with which she could mold. She could turn me into the man that dad never materialized into. My life was nothing more than a test case, a piece on a chessboard. A smaller bit used to wage a larger battle.

Dad, for all his faults, made the most of what he had. He provided for his family and got things done, even if mom didn't like the way he went about it sometimes.

She had no doubt fallen in love with another man, a younger, mythological image of my father. He was big and healthy, full of charm and self-confidence. This was before his drinking turned regular, before his waist expanded as rapidly as his hairline receded. Sure, it seemed superficial but it was tangible and drastic. Mom had been sold a bill of goods and now with me as the result of their marriage she couldn't refund it. Her expectations hadn't been met. This sense of unspoken regret bounced off every corner of the house. It grew with every small paycheck, served as a reminder of what the man of the house could have been.

This failure could be heard in the silence that overtook the room whenever I walked in. Pieces of arguments overheard while around the corner, still out of sight. Fragments of different points of view tested against the other. It was all one big fight, one large struggle and my presence was at the heart of it. But it took this prolonged homebound episode for me to grasp its severity.

The details, the thought behind those halted arguments, came to light a year ago deep in the back of dad's closet.

I had the day off from school, home alone. Boredom led me on a blind scavenger hunt. The papers were the main discovery. That and the vintage Playboys which were sealed. The papers were tucked away in shoeboxes and folders. They were haphazardly stacked together. There was a layer of dust on the papers. The edges had curled in on themselves. A tint of yellowish brown had invaded the top pages of every pile.

Most of them were dated on the top right corner like a school assignment. The only common thread was that they were written before my birth. I hadn't seen my dad so much as write down a grocery list in all the years since.

The most recent paper I could find was scribbled, as if the hand couldn't control itself to one word at a time. There was just enough time to skim through it. I rushed through sentences, skipped lines, and scoured the pile for mentions of myself. Dad would be home soon. I'd have time to analyze the words later.

The pieces that stood out were confessions. They read as if dad thought his words had a sense of immunity to them. No one was exempt from his tirade. The words wife and baby bounced off the page. My hands shook and my stomach tightened.

Mistake, disappointment, and a lack of a future littered the pages. It was more complex than him being scared of fatherhood. It was the other boxes of papers, abandoned bank forms for a business loan and half finished floor plans of a store that carried more weight. They were written out on bar napkins and in the margins of the local newspaper. The plans were vague thoughts cobbled together.

It was a part of some bigger, grander future, one that didn't have room for me in it.

That night awake in bed, I rehashed the contents of the documents. Part of me was annoyed with my dad because he viewed me as a nuisance, another mouth to feed. My anger was unable to turn into concrete rage. The distance between the letters and myself were too great. Too much time had passed. Another part of me was full of embarrassment and pity. How could a man use something like a child as an excuse to give up on his goals? He was young, 18 at the time, but this image of my dad as a vulnerable young man clashed with the mythical stoicism shaped by his quiet and steady attitude that I knew.

He was a man-child. He brooded and sulked over a lifetime of regrets. He was never able to come out and say what bothered him. My dad had given me a blueprint on how to conduct myself as a man. But these papers contradicted all of it.

Bad grades? Work harder. Trouble with a school bully? Go right at him, never back down. Unlucky with girls? Eventually they'll come to you and if they don't, then they ain't worth worrying about. Can't make the sports teams? Spend more time practicing. Can't make friends at school? Fuck 'em. School is short; life is long. These were his messages for me and he preached them everyday.

The frustration had to be even more palpable for mom. She caught the brunt of his frustrations. There was nothing simple about their relationship, no enjoyment in each other's company.

I tried to picture the young man my dad once was. The man mom fell in love with. Full of energy and ideas, ready to conquer whatever the world threw his way. Where did that go? Had that youthfulness been sucked up by my arrival? Was it the lower class existence that they were trapped in? Mom would never admit as much and I was too scared to ask.

There weren't many pictures of the two of them when they first met. They were young, too busy to slow down and memorialize individual moments. In the few that I found before they had me they looked so young. Mom looked happy, beautiful, and full of life. Dad looked rugged. He was unshaven with long hair, a cut-off Lynyrd Skynard t-shirt, and a sleeve full of tattoos. But no matter how much dad's physical presence dominated the photos, no matter how much he dwarfed mom, my eyes focused on her. She held him tight, arms around his waist as if she were scared that if she let go he'd leave.

The one picture that got my attention was the two of them in front of the house. They had just bought it. Dad held the "Sold" sign in his hands. Mom, right by his side, was huge, pregnant with me. Mom's look of joy was absent. She looked worried, uncertain. The spark in her eyes long gone, her cheeks were pale and her hair looked like it hadn't been cut or done up in months. She had bags under her eyes; like a prizefighter the morning after a grueling bout. It looked as if it took all her energy just to stand up on her feet for the photo. She didn't hold him tight. It was a small, but noticeable shift. Mom played the role of her new character: happy wife. She looked tired. Her forehead glistened with sweat.

Dad looked equal parts terrified and excited. I could make out the muscles in his forearms as he gripped the sign tight. That was his proof that he made it as a man. That sign verified that he was able as a provider and head of the family. It looked like he was going to bend the sign in half.

This photo, this memory, was the pinnacle of their youthfulness and it made me want to cry. After that it was all-nighters spent by my crib side and the factory and mortgage bills that never stopped. Adult life had punched them right in the mouth.

I held onto the photo with both hands, took it out of the frame, and ran my fingers across it. The edges were worn. A wrinkle ran through the middle of it, which made its way right in between my parents. The subtle irony of it had gone unnoticed for all these years.

I fell asleep that night with a different view of dad. I didn't respect quite as much. He'd given up, laid down, and settled for us. We were his back-up plan, daily reminders of the path he'd chosen not to take.

The next morning dad left for a few hours. He went to supply the house with enough stuff to keep mom off his back. I imagined him as he cursed at inanimate objects on his way to the store, unable to vent his frustration over the classic rock radio station run by the local state college. No doubt with a cigarette in his mouth, raspy throat, lungs filled with phlegm as he powered through the elements in a bullish way. If something inside of me didn't fear that my future was destined to mirror his than I would've laughed.

He'd already caved in once before since this thing had started. He purchased a new snowplow from some small auto body shop. The guy claimed it was new. Dad didn't mind the fact that it was already on the owner's rig. The details were fuzzy, like most things with dad. The guy told him that he didn't need it until Thanksgiving and then after that they'd talk about it. Dad never told me what he paid for it. The struggle, the fight to equip his vehicle for battle against this thing, was what he relished most.

Mom came down, lit a candle, sat down on the couch, and started to read a trashy romance novel. It was her release, her brief respite from the daily reminders of her boring life. I judged her from afar. Stared at her in her old sweatpants and moth-hole riddled robe and wondered where she gave up. Did she want to be the woman on the cover? The constrictive, reinforced stereotype of the weak woman in need of a strong, male savior was too easy a path for her to take. She was smarter than that. She made me want to get up, go over, and rip that blatant signal that she wasn't satisfied with her life out of her hand and bury it deep in the white outside, next to the blood of the dead worker. Instead I sat there and wondered when I'd give in to my fate, my lack of a future, and become a replica of my parents.

Dad got back by mid afternoon. He was drunk. He parked the truck into an ice bank, closer to our front door than the shoveled out section of the driveway. As he backed up I saw his eyes from the house. The darkness didn't matter. The snow couldn't hide his eyes as they hovered a few feet above the steering wheel. He looked like he had rabies, infected with a lethal blend of whiskey and anger. He used the plow to break through the mound of hardened snow. He didn't have the patience to try and maneuver his old truck into the driveway.

He threw the front door open, hands full of boxes and bags.

"Shit ain't gonna carry itself," he said.

I trudged through the front yard with him, connected by our common struggle against nature.

"Throw all the liquid in a pile of snow by the house. Make sure to jam a stick in place so we don't lose it."

Milk, beer, whiskey, and orange juice were put away like Easter eggs before a hunt.

I lugged in two boxes of battery-powered space heaters, careful not to drop them. Mom was in the living room. She had already begun to open stuff, rummaged through the boxes like a squirrel at the base of a tree.

"Be easy with it and make the stuff last. Cost me $1,000."

Mom froze at the mention of the amount.

"Wouldn't have cost a penny to go to my sister's house," she said.

"What?"

"Just saying that we can't maintain this."

"We?"

"Don't start with me, not today. I'm not in the mood," she said.

Dad ignored her. He was more concerned with the supplies he had bought. He wanted to take it all in, bask in his momentary triumph. Hidden beneath the whiskey stupor was a gleam of pride. Amongst the supplies there was a purpose in his eyes. For the first time in a while he was needed.

"Getting any better out there?"

"Worse actually," he said.

Dad didn't even look up from the supplies. Mom waited for him to explain, but dad would rather have handed her his bi-weekly checks and cut out the need for a conversation. His information, his description, would have to satiate her desire. She'd never been so anxious to hear the variations of black, gray, and white before. Her eyes remained fixed on him. She wanted him to fill in the details. He was her sole link to the outside world. Like a hungry predator on the prowl for more nourishment, she needed something out of him. Something she refused to take from my last trip outside. She knew dad could handle the destruction around him.

"Power's out everywhere and the roads haven't been plowed in days."

She exhaled, disappointed. She wanted, needed, more, something to quench her thirst. Mom gave up after an hour of back and forth one-sentence answers. She moved on, ripped through the groceries in the kitchen like a stoned teenager. She pouted like a child.

Dad motioned me over, waited for me to get within earshot. The sense of pride had left his eyes. All that was left was a mixture of the alcohol and something else, something I'd never seen before. It looked like he was afraid, scared of what he'd seen. I knelt down and took in the toxic fumes that came off his breath. In the small space of silence between us, the wheezy moans of his lungs produced the only noise in the house.

Mom sulked past us, box of Twinkies in hand. She stomped up the steps and slammed the bedroom door behind her. Dad looked outside, through the curtains. It didn't matter that he couldn't make out anything specific. The act was out of character, wasn't the man I knew. It was contemplative.

Gone was his usual aggressiveness. The wrinkles were more pronounced around his eyes, chin, and across his forehead. He didn't have it in him to admit that he had already given up, if just a bit. His powerlessness over the situation frightened me.

He snapped out of it a few minutes later.

"Sit down and listen," he said. "It's about outside."

I kept quiet; I didn't want to ruin the moment. Dad needed to share what he saw, to unburden himself somehow.

Dad spoke of what he'd seen that day. His descriptions of the silent devastation that surrounded us were rhetorical long and detailed. His words gave life to the stillness outside. He animated this thing. His words hid a mix of tolerance and guilt over inaction and powerlessness that he'd never verbalized to me before.

He spoke in a confessional tone, began to reconstruct the outside world, as he now knew it. He was my lens, my channel to everything out there. I hung on every word, trusted in his ability to leave out the unneeded information. He started slowly at first and picked up steam as he continued. He morphed into a spoken map, a chronicle of our town's despair.

It was the first time that he spoke to me at length without a drink in hand or out of anger.

He said that our yard wasn't that bad. Our block, though, was in the middle of the storm. Neighbor's houses were obscured behind piles of snow and broken tree limbs. He said they resembled child made back-yard forts.

Not a single power line remained on our street. Yards looked like the front lines of a war. The snow, which was cleared before the death, cre-ated a giant hill that ran the length of our street, like a wall of sorts. We were hidden from the street, safe from enemy fire. But our enemy didn't spray bullets. It dropped dense, white grenades from the sky.

Dad couldn't see our house from the street. The only things in his view were the few older, sturdiest groups of trees that hadn't yet col-lapsed. The only house still visible from the street was the top floor of a three-story house at the end of the block. Dad said their roof had given in, caved to the pressure of the storm. A giant hole, half the size of the roof, made the home unlivable. He said that it looked like a bomb had been dropped. A path was still evident from the driveway to the street. They'd given up, fled to safer ground. Dad's voice trailed off at the men-tion of this exodus. He didn't want mom to overhear him.

Dad confirmed my suspicions. I couldn't imagine another street being hit as hard as ours. Not with the death, which had become the first con-firmed fatality of this thing.

He spoke of his plow, the only thing of any value that he owned out-right, and how it struggled to break through the layers of ice that had formed from days of inattention. I didn't have the heart to point out that the plow was due back in a few months. As our town's DPW shut down, the remnants from the storm had piled up, inch by inch. It proclaimed its victory over us. The workers quit out of fear of being the next casualty.

As dad struggled outward, off of our block, desolation reigned supreme. Causing drifts, only gusts of wind blew the snow. Everything else was boarded up or abandoned. The usual two-minute drive to the main road took him half an hour.

The main road, a two-lane extension of the back streets, was just as treacherous. Dad said he passed four cars broken down on the side of the road. Once he reached the town's limits, a few news vans were parked on the grassy hill, safely away from our everyday burden of snow and ice. A man with a camera ran up to dad as he stopped at the four corners, which was the boundary between our winter and every-one else's summer. He didn't even roll down his window as the reporter stuck out his microphone. As the light turned green dad flipped him the middle finger and sped off into the dry streets in front of him.

So much change in such a little amount of space and time. Dad couldn't comprehend it. He downed half the flask of whiskey from his middle console before he got to the superstore. I didn't know why he told me, why he thought it important. He skipped parts of his journey, like what he'd done to mom earlier but in a different way. He didn't hold back on me but he shielded me in a way. He told the story his way, selfish and possessive.

After the talk of the snow went away I didn't listen as intently. Part of me wanted stories of blood and squalor, something to press against my own experience of death in order to numb it. He went on about the lines at the store and how everything that was available was marked up in price. He went on a rant about large corporations, how they took jobs and killed local businesses, how it wasn't fair that these companies could manipulate the masses like puppets and make us pay whatever they deemed fit.

"They have us by the balls kid and most of us are too dumb to even realize it," he said.

He said that the trip home was much quicker. Not because the roads got any better but because he was fueled by anger over being taken advantage of in his desperation.

"Makes you wonder if there's an honest man out there," he said.

I didn't know how to respond. It wouldn't sound genuine. What did I know about fairness and honesty and corporations and grown up things? My main purpose was to serve as the buffer between his rage and mom's apathy. My quietness and obedience, my distance from dad, was the only way to accomplish that.

Dad went out to the garage without a word. Mom was at my side by the time he flung our front door open. The wind had picked up. Snowdrifts came into the house.

"Let's go," he said.

There was a metal ladder by his side, half obscured by the snow.

"Where?"

"Just follow me," he said.

Mom saw the ladder and got anxious.

"Wait a second. What are you up to?"

"Gonna clean the roof off," he said.

"In this weather? That's crazy!"

"Someone's gotta make sure the roof don't collapse in under us."

"Well you're not bringing my baby up there with you. He's been through enough without you putting him on the roof in the middle of a blizzard," she said.

"It's a two man job. Not all of us can sleep all day hoping this storm goes away."

"You know what? Fuck you! If you want to play hero knock yourself out but if Wilson gets hurt don't bother coming down from there," she said.

Dad grunted, lit a cigarette, and looked at me.

"Ready?"

"Sure," I said.

"Hurry up, you're tracking in a bunch of snow," she said.

She whispered "take care of yourself" as I closed the front door behind me.

Dad looked at me. His beard was already white with snow and beginning to stiffen like ice. His nose was bright red, his cheeks flush from popped blood vessels, and his eyes were glossed over. They had a little fight, somewhere deep down, left in them.

We shoveled for an hour to get fifty feet. Dad ripped the shovel from my hands and plowed through the remaining path to the garage. Dad's patience had worn thin by the time he realized that the garage door handle was frozen shut. Dad sighed, took a step back, and aimed the shovel at it. He cocked it back like a spear. One quick, violent motion and the door handle broke off into multiple pieces. The metallic rust speckled over the pile of snow. It was covered up by new flakes; just like everything else.

A clear path about two feet wide went through the middle of the room. It snaked its way around piles of metal and wood. Dad knew where to find everything he needed. He dove into a pile off to the side and came up with an extra shovel and some more flashlights.

We were outside again, in the middle of the storm, without a word spoken between us. Dad led the way with me close behind. He dragged the ladder through the front yard. My lungs were heavy by the time we reached the side of the house.

The wind had picked up. It was the type of gust that made you squint your eyes. It chilled my bones, bit at my extremities, and shook my core. Dad moved slow and deliberate. He extended the ladder and slammed it against the house. I didn't know if it was due to the weather or because he was mad. Mom ducked her head out the living room window. She tightened her robe close to her chest as she caught her first breath of the outside air.

"What the hell's going on?"

"Shut up!" Dad yelled.

Mom said something to herself before she pleaded with us to be careful. It was directed more towards me but dad rolled his eyes and grunted. His eyes remained focused on the ladder.

"Mind your damn business and close the window."

"Whatever," she said.

She slammed the window shut.

"You're going up first. I'll be fine on my own."

"Okay," I said.

"Just take the flashlights with you and I'll bring the rest."

"Sounds good."

"When you get up there you'll be unprotected from the wind. Take a few steps in to the middle and sit down and wait. Okay?"

This was the way he showed fatherly affection. The question at the end was for show and wasn't negotiable.

Fear rushed over me as my second foot clinked onto the ladder. I was no longer bound to the cold, snow covered Earth, I was reliant on some old rusty metal. Every sound, sight, and smell was amplified. I could hear my dad as he blew into his curled up hands to keep warm, a bird as it swooshed through the air separated from his flock, a stray cat as it pawed through the slushy street.

My pulse spiked, blood surged through my veins. Clouds of breath obscured my vision. Beads of cold sweat lathered my face. A buffer between my skin and countless layers, dampness swooshed around underneath my clothes.

I stopped to look down for a moment and almost lost my balance. My father's neck was jerked upwards as he watched my every move. He guided me with his hands upward. He lifted me by will, hoped that mom's worries wouldn't come to fruition.

I was chest level with the roof but still needed to take another few steps to the very top of the ladder to have a chance at the roof. The top step was slick with snow. My right foot sunk into the snow immediately. Now I was knee deep, straddled between the ladder and the roof.

Dad yelled something up to me. Probably encouragement in the form of an order. I jumped sideways onto the roof like those skaters on TV that braced for a fall after they tried a trick. My back hit the surface and broke through the initial iced layer with a loud crunch.

I was submerged in snow. My back had hit against the house, which was pitched at a slight angle. I had to punch my way back up to the surface and flashed the light to let him know it was okay.

I wanted to scurry back to the edge and watch dad make the same climb but with all that extra gear. But the frozen edge, slick with a coat of ice, scared me, kept me in place. I squatted like a catcher, waited, and looked around. The clouds hung low. There was so much nothingness. Boring, monotonous colors began to blend. It was pale and desolate, like the painter had run out of color and continued with gray, black, and white. Everything was covered in a blanket of dirty, crusty white snow. Mailboxes scattered in the street, far from their original place, plastic shopping bags swirled around like that scene from that weird movie about the dad in a mid-life crisis.

This gray mist was draped over our town like a dirty tablecloth. We were the unfinished wooden table, splinters and all. I used to dream about being able to fly, thought it would be so cool to be amongst the clouds. Now, as the clouds closed in on top of me, the ground was my dream setting.

Dad's hand was the first thing visible. The sound as he pawed at the roof's edge startled me. He yelled something and then the two shovels were airborne. They landed a foot in front of me. One made a dull thud; the other hit the snow, metal first, like a javelin. My thoughts went to the dead worker. The snow on the roof turned blood red for a few moments. Dad hopped onto the roof like a cat, oblivious to the weather.

"This ain't gonna clear itself. Work from the middle out."

The snow was heavy. As quickly as a path was cleared new flakes covered it up. Dad grunted and moaned behind me. He was bent over at the hips, shovel in constant motion, faster and faster. He was done in half the time it took me.

"Come on already," he said.

He helped me with my side. It was more of a get out of my way than assistance. He opened his jacket and took out a folded up tarp. He unraveled it, let it fall to the surface, and gave the roof one last quick sweep.

"Take one end and spread it out to the edge. We're lucky the roof hasn't already started leaking."

He handed me a few nails and told me to wait on my side until he was done. He pulled a hammer out of his back pocket and nailed down his side. He slid the hammer to me. I followed his lead. The wind whipped up, caught the tarp and lifted it. It looked like we had assembled a make-shift tent. With each flake the tarp began to fall to the surface, weighed down by this thing.

Dad went down first. He skipped onto the top step of the ladder. A few steps down I heard a noise and saw his hands grasp for the edge of the roof. His head popped up.

"Forgot the fucking shovels and hammer."

He got hold of the hammer and tossed it over his shoulder without hesitation, or even a look. He did the same with the shovels but because of their length and weight he had to rotate his torso and drop them down. With the second one out of his hand he slipped from the ladder and followed the tools towards the ground.

The only sound was the thump-thump from the second shovel as it hit the ground followed by him. He landed on his back. Not a sound out of him. I crept to the edge for a better look. The snow had started to fall on his limp body. His eyes were wide open.

I yelled down. Not quite to him but at him. I was scared. Scared about what waited for me on the ground. Scared to go back down the ladder. Scared to stay put and do nothing. The screams continued, as loud as possible.

The front door flung open and then slammed shut. Mom's voice soon followed.

"Wilson? Where are you guys? What happened? Are you alright?"

"It's dad. He fell!"

A moment later her screams overtook mine as she found dad in the snow pile. She was crouched over, hands hovered, scared to touch him, injure him further.

"Be careful sweetie." With every step down the ladder mom squealed out in terror. "Easy does it, don't rush," she repeated.

"He's not responding!" She yelled.

"Alright, look you're going to freeze out here." With both feet on the ground my mind was clear. "Go start the truck and wait inside for it to warm up. I'll carry him over and we'll go to the hospital."

There was no time to think, just go. I, we, had to be quick and decisive for the first time in weeks. This thing had dulled my mind; ground me to a near stand still.

Dad moaned in pain. Mom screamed; her nerves frayed.

I'd driven before, dad let me fool around in the school parking lot a year earlier but that was different. There were no mounds of snow, no sheets of ice, just pavement and his watchful eye to guide me.

I slammed on the gas, looked back over my shoulder, and the truck jerked forward. We stopped only a few inches from the garage. Now the front tires were up on a snow bank. Mom looked at me, then darted her eyes to the gearshift. She didn't blink until she saw that it was in reverse. Another go at it on the gas, this time no dramatic shift just a deep sound like I had revved the engine in park. Mom rolled down the window and looked out. The tires motion wore down the snow until we got to level ground. A loud drop and then we shot backwards out halfway into the street before the brakes caught onto the surface.

"What the fuck is going on?" Dad yelled.

"Enough, you're not helping the situation!" Mom said.

I lowered the plow and bent the wheel hard right. Cleared the few cars parked on the street by a foot and had a straight shot for a mile. Off in the distance the horizon melted together, the snow and ice became inseparable from the clouds and sky. The toughest part was to find a reference point to guide me along the way. My boundaries for the first few blocks were the downed power lines. Thick black cords draped over trees and on top of car shaped snow piles. With no one else on the road I could afford to guide the three of us this way. We sloshed about from side to side on the road.

I was scared to stop the truck, worried that it would get stuck in the snow, but terrified that we'd gain too much speed and wouldn't be able to stop. We'd become a land barge, in search of that proper balance, that perfect speed. Mom clutched her seat, hands turned white from pressure applied every time I hit the gas.

We rolled through the stop signs, hopeful that traffic wouldn't get in our way. For the first few blocks it wasn't a problem. The lack of cars, the complete absence of any signs of life, was both convenient and creepy. It felt like those scary movies I'd watch with mom as dad worked the night shift. The ones where everything was quiet and still right before the killer appears and starts his rampage. I waited for background music, the soundtrack, to fade away and the bloodshed to begin. It wasn't rational, didn't make sense, but nothing about this summer did.

My chest was tight and my body still stung. I slowly thawed out from the change in temperature. By the time the heater pumped warmness fully, we were halfway to the hospital. We were free from the storm. Just like that, like someone had turned on stadium lights overhead. No warning, just bright and warm. Now we baked under the foreign rays of the sun. I rolled the window down, anxious to feel the warm summer breeze against my face. The humidity hit my frozen pores and softened my face. Cheeks red and flush, I concentrated on this new land.

The hopelessness inside the truck was overwhelming. My eyes avoided the rearview mirror; it was too sad of a sight. I couldn't turn my head to the right either; mom was a mess. The motor rumbled and gurgled just enough to drown her out.

Mom had never cried like that before. And not just for dad. She was sad about our dilapidated house, depressed about her once slim figure turned to another casualty of her domestication, miserable that her paycheck was enough to make her count down the days until the next meager one, gloomy about the fact that the love of her life had turned into her father, with each swill of whiskey his waist expanded and his gut protruded over his worn belt, unhappy that she had been complicit in the events that led to her current place. But those tears, those dabs at the corners of her eyes, were isolated, shushed and hidden as much as they could be. This was different. This was guttural, instinct driven, and uncensored. With her tears came a continuous scream that pierced through the truck and rang through my head.

Her tears went silent as we got closer to the hospital. The flowers were in full bloom and the kids wore shorts. I focused on the colors, all of them. Broad strokes of green brushed across the landscape only miles from our front door. A crystal clear blue sky was above us, limitless off into the distance. My eyes were teased with its vibrancy. The pavement was black; free from weeks of hard rain, snow, ice, and sleet. The double yellow line, something that had disappeared weeks ago, popped off the road like a three-dimensional art piece.

It was all so beautiful yet right behind me, inches away from me, was such horror. It was good to have gained temporary freedom from the darkness but dad's life, his fight to keep it, overshadowed everything.

We caught every green light and I was able to let the truck loose on the solid ground beneath us. Mom turned her attention to dad in the back-seat. They whispered amongst themselves. Her quiet assurances went unheard as he slipped in and out of consciousness. It was the longest they'd been together without an argument since the first flake of snow appeared. This was what it took, an injury, the threat of nonexistence, for them to be kind to each other. Dad's injury made him vulnerable. Mom saw a path and took it. She relished the opportunity to try and connect with him, regardless of the circumstances. It didn't matter that he was barely conscious.

I honked the horn and skidded to a stop, two wheels up on the curb in front of the Emergency Room entrance. Mom gasped for air as the truck slammed into park. Nobody came out to meet us. They must've been trained to only answer ambulance sirens. Mom took the keys and went to park the truck as I threw dad's arm over my shoulder and helped him inside. Nobody looked up as the automatic doors slid open. Everyone was in their own rush to put out the next fire.

"I need some help here! My dad, he fell off a ladder. He's unconscious."

My voice had gone back to that weird early puberty phase full of cracks between levels, somewhere between boy and man. Unable to compose myself, I couldn't form full sentences.

Dad collapsed into an empty wheelchair. I banged on the front desk desperate for attention. A lady looked up at me briefly and motioned with her index finger to hold on. She finished her phone call and then asked for my name. I rambled off a variation of what I'd pronounced moments ago. She looked over my shoulder at my dad, then back to me before she cut me off.

"You're going to have to fill this out. Right now we're full. I'll page an-other nurse and see if we can get him set up with a bed in the back soon. Just be patient. I'll call you when we're ready."

The hospital was busy. People were everywhere. Uniforms ran back and forth with a frantic purpose in their eyes. The intercom hummed with a constant barrage of voices that directed different doctors to certain wings of the five level building.

It had been five years since we were last in this hospital. I'd broken my arm during a game of tackle football with a bunch of kids from the neighborhood. They went and got my mom, who was home from work, and she took me to the hospital. That's when we still had a second car, hers. Dad met us after his shift ended. He leaned in and gave me a half hug, not quite sure what to do with his hands. He smelt like an ashtray and sweat. His hands were black and greasy. Somehow my arm turned into an argument. Dad mad at mom for how much this was going to cost and mom mad at dad for his misguided worry.

The waiting room in the hospital was as full as the main lobby but much more quiet and reserved. It was even cool. They pumped air conditioning through the place in response to the recent heat wave. Mom and I were still wrapped up in several layers. We looked misplaced. There were only a few others bundled up like us. They had the same tired look in their eyes. Dark circles wrapped around their eyes like pieces of coal. Also not used to the light, we squinted in silent unison. Disheveled, they looked like they should be on the other side of the hospital wall. I shuddered to think what their injured loved ones looked like. There were quite a few others like dad that sat and waited in pain. Some injuries were visible, others weren't. People clutched their sides, eyes shut. Others had homemade bandages that covered up open wounds.

A man in scrubs called my dad's name. He stared at paperwork on a clipboard as dad sat inches from him. My entire dad boiled down to a few pages. He asked me a few questions about the fall and then turned dad around and wheeled him back behind closed doors. I stopped them, told the man that he didn't understand, that that was my dad; that he needed to get better. He said to be patient. It was the second time I'd heard that word in a half an hour; that someone would come back out when they know more. I stood there as dad disappeared into the labyrinth of the hospital and wondered if there was any connection between the staff's constant use of the word patience when they dealt with patients.

We waited. Mom sat next to me, mute. Her hands fidgeted, right knee tapped up and down against the cold tiled floor. The lights above us were bright; teased us with their mere appearance. Neither of us had seen light in weeks. Now they blinded us, didn't allow us to see through the door and down the hallway to where they took dad. The television in the corner drowned out my thoughts, my worries, about dad. A soap opera played. The daytime scripted drama had an audience but ours had no one. The news stations had moved on to bigger events, ones that affected more influential people than us. A few local news trucks still roamed our dark streets.

"He's going to be okay," My eyes were still fixed on the television screen.

"Is he?"

"He's tough, he'll bounce back."

"Okay," she said.

There was nothing left to say. Mom didn't want to talk. My mind wandered; the further away from the hospital the better. The moment was too big, felt like it had the ability to swallow me whole. His injuries, his accident had taken mom hostage. That wasn't going to happen to me. I was tied to them out of circumstance not choice and knew that one day my future wouldn't include them. Mom chose this; it was too late for her. She had hitched herself to dad. I'd be free soon enough. There was still a chance of something better for me.

I went to the cafeteria. Mom looked at me blankly, unable to verbalize the fact that her stomach was upside down, that her insides had twisted themselves into a knot. A slice of pizza had eluded me for weeks, thoughts of a cheeseburger appeared in my mind like a mirage. I grabbed a handful of food, took a corner seat in the busy café, and ate quickly. It didn't matter that people watched me stuff my face. Chunks of food and gulps of cold fountain soda was my act of rebellion in response to this accident.

When I got back to the waiting room mom was gone. So too were the few others dressed like myself. A sea of shorts and sandals were in front of me. The roomful of eyes was focused in on me.

"I'm looking for my mom. She was here a minute ago. We're waiting for my dad."

"What's the name?"

"Hart, he came in a few hours ago."

"They're working on him now. He's up in Room 342. Take the elevator to the third floor, make a right and it'll be halfway down the hall."

The lady didn't even look up from her computer screen. She'd probably learned long ago not to make eye contact, that it was too much of an emotional investment. It was much easier to hide behind the screen of numbers and names. Those didn't die, they just changed.

Mom and dad were in the middle of a conversation when I walked in. By the time the door shut behind me they went quiet. Mom got up and came towards me. Her mascara dripped down her cheeks. No more tears, she had moved on to worry. She gave me a concerned look. It was the same look she'd carried around day after day since this thing hit us. The same glazed over eyes that she had when her boss told her not to come back to work.

"Hey buddy, come here. Say hi to your pops."

"He's hopped up on pain killers sweetie," mom whispered.

"Hey dad."

"What's with the long face? You didn't think a fall would be the end to your old man did you? I've got a little more fight in me than that."

"I know dad. It's good to see you awake."

Dad's arms were weak and loopy around my torso. Gone was his bear hug. I had to wipe away the drool from the side of my face.

"I love you," he said.

"Me too."

He smiled up at me from the bed. He looked out of it.

The only sounds in the room came from the machines hooked up to dad. Beeps and buzzes, they were all different and clashed against one another. It added up to one larger sound. Dad had wires and tubes in each arm and one in his nose. Every few minutes the strap around his arm tightened and took his blood pressure. At first it sounded like a sonar from a submarine. An alarm went off sporadically. It scared me at first. It sounded like something had broke, as if dad was damaged. The noises came and went. Acclimation was fast, like the dark and cold back home. Mom was on the edge of her seat. She kept her eyes fixed on the screen that punched out neon green numbers that flashed like a stock price against its black background.

Mom leaned back into the corner. She looked exhausted. She fumbled around with the television remote for a while. The screen instructed her to pay a service fee. She cursed under her breath and tossed the remote onto the empty bed next to dad.

The doctor came in an hour later. Mom jumped up out of her seat. She was happy to have someone new to talk to. She'd studied all of the charts on the wall. Basic first-aid instructions and other medical posters written in bland language only kept her attention for so long. She didn't want to miss his diagnosis and instructions. She knew that if she didn't hear them that dad would downplay the whole thing.

"Mr. Hart you're a very lucky man. Besides breaking your leg, you suffered a contusion to the back of your head, a concussion, and some minor neck damage. I'd like to keep you overnight to run some final tests. Make sure you don't have any serious brain injuries."

"Is that a possibility?" Mom asked.

"Well since he was unconscious for a while there's a chance that he could've sustained some trauma. So far the initial test results have come back good. We'll know more in the morning."

"Great, thanks doc," dad said.

Mom nodded at the doctor, not quite sure what to add. He looked at her with the emotion of a stranger. Mom wanted to prolong his presence, to hear his voice, his expertise. She knew, we all knew, that once he left the room we'd be stuck with our own morbid thoughts.

"A nurse will check in throughout the night. Visiting hours end at ten but since he suffered a concussion I'm going to ask that you stay with him and make sure he doesn't fall asleep. Can you do that?"

Mom nodded.

"Great, I'll be back to check on you in the morning Mr. Hart. Take care."

"You got it," dad said.

Dad saluted him. He missed his temple and poked himself in the eye. I laughed. Mom turned red with embarrassment.

Mom got up and paced the room. She slid back and forth along the tiled floor like an impatient child. Dad watched her as she stirred, his neck moved like he was at a tennis match.

"Cut it out! You're making me dizzy," he said.

She mumbled something incoherent before she sat back down in her seat.

She was asleep within an hour. The day's events had gotten the best of her. Even though I knew she wanted to stay awake, to make sure dad had everything necessary, she needed her sleep more. Besides, dad wouldn't ask for help anyway. They would just irritate each other; get under each other's skin. Mom wanted to help but she was powerless.

I grabbed a blanket and pillow from the nurse's station and made mom as comfortable as possible. She didn't even move. She looked peaceful with the blanket tucked up beneath her chin.

"And then there were two," dad said.

"Yeah."

"Come on over and take a seat next to me."

"How are you holding up?"

"I'm fine, great actually. The stuff they've got me is better than a bottle of booze," he said.

"As long as you're comfortable. You know you scared mom there for a minute."

"What about you?"

"What?"

"You heard me. No doubt mom was gonna get emotional. How are you doing?"

"I'm fine," I said.

"Good, that's good," he said.

He leaned his head back. No doubt tired from the day. I had to shake him awake as he began to drift off. I wanted to give in and let him have what he wanted. If it were only that simple. These past few months nothing was easy.

We watched each other for a while. He stared at me, foggy eyed from the stream of morphine pumped into him.

"What are you doing?" he asked.

"Just looking. Trying to take in all the lights out there," I said.

The parking lot below was filled with cars. Lampposts illuminated their tiny metallic exteriors. It looked like a floor of bugs, scared to move under the watchful eye of the lights, too late for them to scramble away.

"Stop it, you're freaking me out. It's not an aquarium."

He was hard to understand, forced me to piece together his words. It wasn't even midnight and there was still another seven hours before the hospital got busy enough to keep him awake without my help. I thought about the television, wished it would turn on and drown out everything else. Then we both could relax, I wouldn't have to worry about how to start a conversation with him. We could let others do the hard work for us. Sports, music, news, infomercials; it didn't matter. As long as we could turn off our brains and tune out everything around us.

"Sit down over here," he pointed to the chair next to his bed.

I did as told, hoped that dad would continue with the directions. As long as he carried the conversation, complaints and all, the content didn't matter. The prospect of silence scared me.

"So…"

"What? Out with it already!"

The machines attached to him started to beep louder. His numbers spiked when he spoke.

"Nothing, just…"

He cut me off when he looked up and noticed the television.

"Where's the remote?"

"It won't work unless we pay for it," I said.

"Pay for it? Doc has me up all night and can't even give me something to watch? Go get the nurse."

"They're probably busy."

"Get the nurse or I will," he said.

He was still the bully, even softened with sedatives. I went and found a nurse and told her my dad had a question. I couldn't ask myself, I didn't want to be a burden.

"Well?"

"So, what can I help you with Mr. Hart?"

"Turn the television on," he said.

"Okay, do you know how to operate it?"

"Of course, I'm not an idiot! But I'm not paying for it. Doctor said to stay awake so I need something to keep me awake."

The young nurse looked to me for help. I put my head down, looked at the floor.

"Right, well why don't you talk with your son instead?"

Dad shot me a look like I was a question he couldn't answer.

"For the rest of the night? No, turn it on and charge it to my bill.
You've probably got it all tallied up already anyway. What's another few
dollars?"

Dad had handled the situation better than expected. No curses at least.
He saved that for mom and me.

"Okay Mr. Hart have it your way," she said.

The nurse pulled out a handheld scanner and shinned it onto the bar-
code at the base of the television. A newscast appeared on screen, mid
report. She got the remote and gave it to dad.

"Just try and keep it down. You don't want to wake up your wife."

"Yeah sure," he said.

"Anything else?"

"No."

"Alright well have a goodnight. Try and relax. It'll be morning before
you know it."

Dad nodded, eyes already glued to the screen. The nurse walked out
quietly.

"Alright, that wasn't so hard now was it? Let's see what's on."

I knew we'd watch whatever he chose. My vote would go unnoticed.
This thing didn't change him that much. If anything he might've gotten
even more selfish, more stubborn. I sat back, happy that at least some-

one else would provide the dialogue for the rest of the night.

Dad turned off the news immediately, switched to a sports channel. He mumbled something about how the news didn't give a shit about us.

The pain medication had taken its toll. It made dad have to choose his battles rather than run over anyone or anything that didn't agree with him. Mom was still asleep, the nurse gone. His options were limited. For the rest of the night he gave up, allowed the constant drip of medication to soften him.

He, we, watched highlights from the day of sports. I was amazed not at how much attention these games got but by how many of them there were. Analysis of athletes a handful of years older than me, interviews with coaches, computer generated diagrams parsed as if they held some important secret. They had a touchscreen to draw on, highlighted certain plays. I was confused, angry. Not at this misguided attention but that my dad found it so significant. My attention drifted away from the television and over to dad as he sat mesmerized for the next few hours.

Dad's eyes remained open despite the liquid sleep that ran through him. I turned the television off. Dad stared at a point on the wall in front of him, oblivious to his surroundings. He'd been through two bags worth of pain medication.

The rest of the night went by quickly. The storm had prepared me for times like this. A year ago I couldn't have sat around all night. Now electricity and heat was enough. This thing had lowered my expectations.

As the sun peeked over the horizon dad's eyes widened. They were bloodshot and dry, like worn out sandpaper. His movements were slow. It took him a minute to realize that he wasn't alone.

"What are you doing here?"

"We're in the hospital, we've been here all night."

"I asked you what you're doing here. I'm not stupid," he said.

The morphine had worn off. He'd dripped every last drop from the bag. He was back. I needed mom to wake up. It was too early in the morning to handle him by myself.

"They told us to stay here with you through the night," I said.

"They? Why?"

"Doctor's orders were to keep you awake all night because of your concussion."

"Concussion? If I've been awake all night then tell me why I can't remember a thing?"

"Probably has something to do with that IV in your arm."

"Don't think that because I'm laid up you can start getting fresh with me," he said.

"Sorry, just wait for the doctor to come in. I'm sure he'll have all the answers."

"He damn well better. And I'll tell you another thing, I'm not spending another night here having you watch me like a toddler."

"Okay dad, okay."

Mom woke up, stirred awake by dad's voice.

"What's all the arguing about?" she said.

"Relax, we're talking. You always gotta put your nose in my business?" dad said.

It was uncanny, awake for a matter of seconds and the two were back into mid day form. They were like two boxers who came out of their corners heads down, as they shuffled to the middle of the ring, haymakers being thrown like there hadn't even been a break between rounds.

I took a seat and let mom have a go at him. I was tired from the previous night. Mom looked anxious to take over, like she felt a pang of guilt that she slept through dad's painful night. She hugged him and dabbed his forehead with a wet towel. My abilities were limited to a few hours, to give her some temporary time for herself, a brief respite from being the sole caretaker of our family.

"Wilson go get your mom some breakfast. And pick me up some coffee while you're at it."

"No, sweetie, I'm fine. I'm not hungry. Besides the doctor will be coming soon."

"Well I haven't been sleeping all night," dad said.

He shot her a quick glance but she let it go. I could see that she wanted to say something in response but, like most times, she gave in and let dad have his way. Mom was back to her role of mediator.

When I came back with dad's coffee the two of them were at each other. Their voices were audible in the hallway. A few nurses listened as they huddled by the doorway.

"Excuse me, do you mind?"

They scattered like cockroaches. It made me feel important and intimidating.

"When were you going to tell me? When we were driving home?"

"It's not your problem. I'll deal with it, okay?" dad said.

"You'll deal with it? How? Are you going to try and hit up my sister for another loan?"

The air quotes around loan got my dad to sit up straight in the bed. For a minute he looked like he was going to jump out of the bed and go after her.

I cleared my throat and slammed the door shut, waited for their recognition of my appearance.

"Hey man. You got my coffee? I'm about to pass out over here."

I handed him the coffee and watched as mom slid back into her corner seat. He took the coffee and emptied it with one large gulp. The room was silent for the next hour. Only the overhead speaker that called doctors and nurses to different rooms broke the quietness. Exhausted, I closed my eyes and rested in the corner.

"So how are you feeling Mr. Hart?"

The doctor's words woke me up. The doctor didn't even look at dad.

Something on his chart had his attention. He made his way to the edge of the bed by memory. I remained in the corner, careful not to miss a word but also to not cause attention.

"Tired."

"That's to be expected. Any headaches, blurry vision, confusion?"

"Nothing more than usual," dad said.

The doctor examined dad quickly as if he had other, more important things to attend to. He put away his penlight after he flashed it through dad's eyes.

"Well your vitals are good and the tests all came back clean so we should have you out of here in a little bit."

"Great, anything else?"

"I'm going to give you a prescription for pain relief medication. You should be fine except for the broken leg, which will heal itself in due time. You will need to set up an appointment with your regular physician to have the leg looked at in a few weeks. If you feel any other symptoms with regard to eyesight or headaches get in touch with your doctor immediately. Okay?"

"Perfect."

"A nurse will be in with all the aftercare paperwork and instructions and crutches. Do you need anything else?"

"No, I think you covered it all. Thanks doc," dad said.

"No problem, my pleasure. Have a good day."

And like that he was gone. On to the next appointment, the next patient, the next diagnosis.

"And now we wait…again. You know, a guy could get used to this kind
of setup. Pain meds, meals cooked for you, electricity. All the comforts,"
he said with a slight smile.

Mom was quiet. She wanted more. More out of all of us. More time spent by the doctor on her husband, more seriousness from dad.

The nurse came in with a folder full of papers that we knew dad was going to ignore. She had crutches that were as big as her. A man in a suit and tie followed behind her. He had more papers in hand. He carried himself in a different way, foreign to dad. We could all sense that something important was about to happen.

She came to dad's bedside. The man in the suit stayed in the background, quiet. He waited his turn.

"Okay Mr. Hart I've got everything you need to get you on your way. Just some aftercare: instructions, crutches, and prescriptions. That should do it for me. Do you need anything else?"

"Whose the suit?" Dad asked.

"Oh, he's from the billing department. A formality really, final part of the process before you can go home. I'll leave him to explain it. You take care of yourself and try and stay off the leg as much as possible."

"You got it," dad said.

Dad eyed the suit with skepticism as he approached the bed.

"So, Mr. Hart like the lady said I'm from billing and I'm going to go over the charges with you. Discuss payment options, insurance, and what not."

"Can I choose what not?"

"Excuse me?"

"Out of the three choices I'll take what not. The other two sound expensive," dad said.

Another dopey smile was on dad's face. Mom gasped, shrugged, and looked down at her feet.

"Oh, well yeah," the man laughed awkwardly. "Anyway, here is a complete breakdown of the services and charges connected with them."

He handed dad a pile of papers. Dad flipped through them quickly, scanned for numbers.

"$19,000! What the fuck happened yesterday?"

"Sir, if you look at it again you'll see that between the cost of all the tests that we had to perform and you're overnight stay…well, it all adds up."

"Yeah the numbers add up alright," dad said.

"So what insurance provider do you have?"

"Yeah, well that's the thing. You see my coverage lapsed a little while ago. I'll be paying for it myself."

"Oh, okay well that's not a problem at all. I'll need an extra couple of signatures from you and we can set up a payment plan that is as agreeable as possible," the man said.

"Nothing about this is agreeable. Just tell me where to sign."

"Initial and sign on the bottom right of each page. Do you want a little bit of time to go over the papers? I could come back."

Dad scribbled away, as fast as he could, like he could shrug this off. The man's question lingered, unanswered.

"Just signed my life away. Don't suppose I can stay the night and donate an organ or something and call it even?"

"Jesus, stop making a joke out of this. Listen to the man," mom said.

"Was anyone talking to you?"

It was best not to answer these types of questions.

"No, that's alright ma'am. I'm used to it. I've got the worst job in the whole building. No one is ever happy with me."

"Ma'am? How old do you think she is?"

"Don't answer that! Ignore him, the pain meds are making him woozy," mom said.

"Don't speak for me! I'm perfectly fine and clear headed."

"Okay, well the hospital has plenty of payment plan options for you. Take a look and choose whichever meets you're needs best. Like I said if you need more time…" he trailed off, unsure of himself.

Dad looked at the paper. He had a confused look on his face. His lips moved as he read to himself.

"Time ain't gonna pay any of this. I'll go with the third option."

"Great, very well then. Just sign where marked and I'll give you duplicates of everything for your records and then you can be on your way."

"Fantastic," dad said.

"Do you have any questions for me?"

"Nope."

"Okay, well I hope your stay with us was satisfactory."

"Yeah, satisfactory. That's the perfect word," dad said.

"Well I'll be in touch when your first payment comes near. Just as a friendly reminder."

"Ha, there's nothing friendly when it comes to money," dad said.

"Oh, I didn't mean…"

"Don't apologize to him. He's busting your balls. It's all he's got," mom said.

She looked at dad with a glare I hadn't seen before. She was beyond upset; this time dad fucked things up real bad. As soon as the door shut mom got up and took the papers from dad. She read through them, tried to see what he'd agreed to.

"I can't believe you. First you give that poor guy a hard time and then you don't even fill me in on how you're going to pay. What's wrong with you?"

"Well other than a busted leg, head injuries, and almost dying nothing, I'm perfectly fine other than that. Besides it's under my name. I'm the one who has to pay up. It's my ass on the line," dad said.

"No, it's all of us! When will you realize that the decisions you make affect all of us?"

I stayed seated. My eyes opened fully. No longer able to hide. Dad was in the wrong but it didn't matter. He never gave up; he was too stubborn.

"When will you realize that you complaining doesn't make any difference?" Dad said.

The medicine had started to wear off. He began to make more and more sense.

"Well if there wasn't a problem to begin with I wouldn't have to complain," mom said.

"Look, that's enough! Alright? I'm sorry. I'm so sorry that this fucking storm came out of nowhere and the plant closed and my insurance went with it. Somehow it's my fault and for that, my dear, I'm eternally sorry!"

Dad stood from the bed to get his pants off the chair and stumbled. He caught himself, took a few steps, and wobbled again. I got to him before he fell.

"Stop, I can do it myself!"

Dad's logic never ceased to amaze me.

"Are you okay?"

Gone was the anger in mom's voice, just like that.

"Yeah, I'm fine," dad said as he sat down.

"Get me some scissors in here!" He yelled to no one in particular.

A nurse appeared at the door a few minutes later with a pair of scissors. Dad was still in his element. Didn't matter where he was; he always took control of his surroundings and made others conform to him.

"Here you go Mr. Hart," the nurse said.

Only one night and he was already known by all the staff. Dad nodded, took the scissors, and cut through one pant leg of his jeans. Got them off at the knee, dropped the scissors on the bed, and nodded his head before he got up and put them on.

The nurse sighed, picked up the scissors, and left without a word.

"Let's go," dad said as he put on his sweater.

I carried his jacket and followed his lead. I remained a few paces behind him in case he fell. He wouldn't want it to look like he needed any help. He already brushed by the wheelchair that was left for him.

"Why don't we go get some nice hot food in the cafeteria? I'm buying. What's the sense in hurrying back to the cold house when we have everything here?"

Mom's optimism, her quick transformation into our family's cheerleader, depressed me. It brought me back to the reality of our situation, of their relationship. The happier she became, the more dad acted out.

Dad grunted and nodded without a word as he plodded ahead towards the elevator.

Mom was all smiles as we entered the cafeteria. We were hobbled but whole, together and out of the house for the first time in weeks. That was enough for mom by this point.

"I'll get you some food. What do you want?"

"Doesn't matter. Just something warm to eat and cold to drink," dad said.

I went with mom in order to avoid more alone time with dad than anything else.

"Isn't this nice? Finally out of the house. Electricity and hot food," mom said.

"Yeah it's good but…"

"What sweetie?"

"Well we can't stay here forever. A lunch isn't going to fix everything," I said.

"You're starting to sound like your father."

"No, I'm just saying. Well, I mean, how are you doing? You know about dad and everything?"

Mom sighed and reached for a hot plate of ready made food. She looked like she wanted to talk, to vent her frustration. She just needed a little push.

"Everything? You know how he gets. It's nothing serious. We'll figure it out. We always do, don't we?"

"Yeah, sure. But I'm asking if you're okay," I said.

She looked surprised, like she hadn't been asked how she felt in a long time. My attention caught her off guard. My persistence, insistence, that she talk, that she had someone who wanted to listen, scared her.

"I'm fine. You're dad scared me for a while there. You know, no matter how much we argue it took something like this for me to realize how much I depend on him. You know that we both love you so much, don't you? He just has a hard time showing it."

"Stop, you're doing it again! I'm asking how you're doing and you go and talk about dad."

"Alright, calm down sweetie. I'm worried about how we're going to pay for all this. It's not like we don't already have enough to worry about. It seems like everything is snowballing into one large pile of shit to be honest. So, how am I doing? Well I'm scared, scared that we won't be able to pay our bills, scared that this storm won't ever stop. And I'm so tired. There doesn't seem to be any break to it. A day off, something," she said.

"Well don't get all excited. I'll take care of dad when we get home, okay? You worry about yourself and the house. I'll keep him off your back. Will that help?"

She had a tear in her eye. Maybe it was leftover from yesterday but she started to cry. People on line in the cafeteria stared at us. I didn't care what they, what anyone, thought anymore.

"When did you become such a grown up? That would mean the world to me," she said.

"No problem. Now let's get him so stuffed with food that he forgets to complain about your cooking," I said.

The reason for my offer was two fold. I wanted to help her out and lighten her load. My dad took her for granted and it was about time that someone else helped out. Another reason though was to keep my distance from dad. Something about his behavior was off recently. He took more risks. Now with the fall, the balance of control looked to have caught up to him. There was enough evidence of what this thing could do since it started. Dad's lack of respect for the power of this thing frightened me, and his stubbornness wasn't going to take me down with him.

"Alright honey here you go. Nice and hot. Eat up."

She sounded more like her own mom now. Dad grunted and started to eat. He shoveled the food down without breaths in between.

"Is it good?"

Another grunt.

"Okay well now that we have some time to relax we should talk."

"About what?"

"Our next move," she said.

"Don't start! We're not going to your sister's. I thought we went over that already. I'm not looking for a handout, especially from family."

"Well we should at least have a plan before we head home," mom said.

She'd switched back from mom of two, to mediator. But now she had something behind her, a bit of inner strength. She had become rejuvenated, no longer prepared to give in to him.

"She's right," I said.

"Oh, well as long as you agree," dad said.

"Oh stop it. It wouldn't hurt us to have an idea of what we're going to do. We can't head back to a dark, cold house and act like nothing's happening."

"That was my plan," dad said.

"What about the hospital bill? And the power?"

"This thing will stop eventually. It has to. We've made it this far, why quit now? Plus how is the hospital going to send us the bill if the Post Office stopped delivering mail weeks ago?"

"It's not quitting to cut your losses and move on. It's called being smart. Practicality may be foreign to you but now's as good a time as any to start. And just because the mail stopped coming for a while doesn't mean they're going to forget about our bill."

With each word mom's strength grew. She began to force herself upon him, into the situation. Confident, she pressed the issue.

"Crazier things have happened," dad said.

"Yeah, like you being delusional enough to think you can wish away this bill! If we, no you, don't come up with something to do than I'm going to my sister's, and I'm taking Wilson with me. I'm serious, I'll do it. It's bad enough that you almost died, you're not going to take us all down with your idiocy."

Mom got up and stormed away. She left the cafeteria in a rush. The people around us were either too tired or worried about their sick loved ones to even look up from their tables.

Dad was in shock. Mom's tone made him realize that this wasn't an empty threat, not this time. She'd had enough and stood up for herself. I felt proud and happy for her but hated the fact that she used me as a pawn. Mom's options were limited though. Dad wouldn't cave in because he loved me, he couldn't stand the thought of living in the house alone. Mom always joked that he couldn't survive on his own. She always had that ace in the hole to play.

Now she had played it. I watched as dad thought out how much work would be involved if she left for her sister's.

"Go get her."

With those three words dad acknowledged how important mom was to him. This was more significant than those other three words that he'd throw in her direction drunkenly or to get her off his back.

Mom made it out to the parking lot. She didn't bother to walk slowly. She didn't expect one of us to come after her. Or maybe she didn't care. She stood there, head arched up towards the sunny, clear blue sky.

"You think we'll ever get this back?"

"Sure, weather comes and goes," I said.

"You shouldn't have to listen to us argue like that. You know that's about your dad, right?"

"Yes."

I wanted to say more, say something profound in that moment to assure my mom that everything was fine. Tell her that she didn't need to worry about me. I didn't need to add on to that list, take up space in her head.

We went back inside. I needed to break up the silence through action but didn't realize that this only made dad's life easier. We got back to him as he tried to hobble out the side exit for a smoke. Five minutes and nicotine had already taken priority over mom. Out of sight out of mind.

"I'm sick of this, okay? Sit down and come to some sort of an agreement. Just figure it out. Is that too much to ask?"

"Relax big man," dad said.

"Oh honey, please calm down. We'll figure something out," mom said.

"Good, because I'm not leaving here until you guys do," I said.

It felt good to have my voice heard. I was energized by mom's stance. In that moment dad had no more sarcastic remarks and mom now looked at me as a young adult. No more jokes, no more sweeties or honeys. Up until now we had always been a family of one, or two at the most. Our priorities and allegiances shifted and morphed on a daily basis. It was either dad as the dictator or mom eager to place me on her side as a two against one offensive.

"Well I'm going for a smoke," dad said.

We took a table outside in the courtyard. Both were too stubborn to speak the first word, to show their hand. Mom had begun to imitate dad's tactics. It was her only shot.

"Alright dad, she's not bluffing. And mom you realize that dad won't be able to live on his own, right? So either we're moving, as a family, or we're staying put for good and riding this thing out."

"I can take care of my goddamn self! Don't speak for me," dad said.

"Stop it! You're willing to let us go, to leave, just to make a point?"

"You don't know nothing about nothing. I'm not trying to make a point, I'm trying to save our house, our life," dad said.

Smoke fumed out of his nostrils like a bull.

"What life? We've got no jobs, no heat, no electricity, nothing," mom said.

"Those things are temporary," dad said.

"Yeah well I'm tired of waiting. And to be clear, if I leave I'm not coming back and I'm not waiting for you. This is it," mom said.

Dad sat and thought about this last statement. He was down to his filter. He lit another one.

"Fine! Alright, okay, we'll move. Happy? But we're not going to your family for help. I'm willing to move but we're doing it on my terms, got it?"

Mom looked at me. She realized this was as much as we were going to get out of him. It didn't matter that he conceded; he still had to hold onto something, some sense of things being done his way.

"Oh baby, thank you. Thank you so much. It's going to be great, for all of us. Just wait and see," mom said.

Tears ran down her cheeks. Dad grunted.

"Can we get out of this place now?"

"Sure, let's go home," mom said.

Mom had won this battle. She'd stood up and defeated him. It took dad a visit to the hospital, but he relented. I think he figured it was better to give in to mom than to death.

I didn't really want to go back home but the hospital was a reminder of dad's mortality. Even though there was electricity the place had an odor of death. Even the colors were too much. My eyes had grown used to the darkness, acclimated themselves to view things through a prism of shadows. The hospital, with its white walls, black and white checkered floor, and cheap reproductions of famous artwork, was sensory overload. The constant noise and traffic of people were at direct odds with our snowy fortress like solitude.

Mom and dad both wanted to get back home, though for different reasons. Dad had grown antsy and as his pain medication began to wear off his grumpiness reappeared. After the financial fiasco and the way the nurses and doctors had spoken down to him, gave common sense instructions like he was an old invalid, dad wanted out. He looked embarrassed, defeated by the past days events. He'd given up and was scared of the possibility that the hospital might find more services to charge him for. He didn't want another so called expert to tell him what to do. Mom wanted to get home and begin the process of our move as quickly as possible. None of us returned home because we missed it. It was a means to a larger end. The possibility of a better, more comfortable, warmer future propelled us back towards the temporary darkness.

We left the hospital overdressed and disheveled. The bright sun beamed down on our ashen faces. My layers of clothes had already stuck to my body with a layer of sweat. Shortly we'd be back in winter but this realization didn't make the transition any smoother. Dad barely used the crutches. Mom got into the driver's seat and flung open the passenger side door from the inside. I helped dad into the backseat, gently at first and then with a shove of frustration.

"I don't need any God damn help!"

He fell onto the backseat on his side. He refused to move or shift himself as if to make a point that he was still self-sufficient. I was too tired to care, I'd already had enough of his childish tantrums and constant need for a battle of some sort. I folded the seat back and hopped in.

Mom, still giddy from her win against dad, smiled at me.

"We all set?"

"Yeah, you good to drive?" I asked.

"Sure sweetie. Don't worry about me."

"Why'd you let me drive here?"

"It all happened so fast. Maybe the cold air froze my brain," she said.

"I wasn't that bad," half declaration, half in search of affirmation.

"No but that's not the point. You're still a boy and you shouldn't have driven. We were lucky nothing happened. But don't get used to it. You still have a few years to wait," she said.

The hospital parking lot was full. I wondered how many of the cars belonged to people who'd return to a warm home. Traffic was slow but we weren't in a hurry. We had nothing to get back to. Everyone else on the road was impatient, in a rush to get somewhere. The beeps of horns were constant until we reached the outskirts of our town. As we approached, the cars thinned out, the sounds muted, the movement around us came to an abrupt halt. The busy hospital halls were a distant memory. There wasn't another car in sight by the time we reached the first dark traffic light.

"What the hell's going on up there? Why we going so slow?" dad moaned from the backseat.

"It's just the weather. Tough sledding," mom said.

"Well get going. That's what the truck is for! Did you even drop the plow?"

"Yes, relax. We'll be there soon enough," I said.

As the words left my mouth I knew it was a mistake.

"Watch your tone or I'll break one of these crutches over your head!"

"Come on guys, can't you get along? Can't even go one day without you two going at it. You're both acting like children," she said.

"What's dad's excuse?"

Dad didn't hear me. I'm not sure if mom did. I had become more like my dad with each day of this storm. The need to get the final word in and to always be ready with a wise remark was the mirror image of him.

Nothing had changed in the neighborhood as we slushed through the streets slowly, methodically. There were a few idle tire tracks from others crazy enough to venture out. Mom locked into one of them and lifted the plow. Within a minute we started to slide back and forth across both sides of the street.

"Put the fucking plow down or stop and let me drive!"

"Okay, okay relax," mom said.

"Hard to when you got me thrashing about like I'm on some county fair ride," he said.

Mom sighed, shook her head, and rolled her eyes. Just between us though, dad couldn't see. Our shared moments, however small, were enough to keep me from a breakdown since we lost power. Our mutual topic was always dad and his quick temper, his general grumpiness. How we bonded, what we shared, wasn't important.

The snow had long ago turned into a dirty mixture of various colors. It was impossible to gauge the gloominess stuck inside the darkness of the house. It all blended together. Bland hues of nondescript colors morphed together into one large dark canvas. Now outside, amongst it, in it, the snow took on a new dimension. It looked old, aged.

Cars parked on the sides of the street were now nothing more than lumps of white powder. It looked like one giant blanket with a few bumps in it. The cars, even the one-story houses, resembled little children hidden under a giant bed cover. The power lines that still stood were hunched over. They looked frail, like a zigzag row of charred toothpicks that poked up from the hard, frozen tundra.

Mom put the plow back down as she tried her best to steer us home. I felt like we were on a ship as it made its way through the ice filled waters of the Bering Sea like in that show my dad always watched. Those fishermen were his version of reality star cowboys, twenty first century John Waynes.

Even with the plow at the head we never got over 15 mph. Our front of the garage, yanked the keys out of the ignition, and jumped out of the car.

The ladder was still against the side of the house. A reminder of our own mortality. We went by it without a word. Dad's body outline in the snow had long ago been replaced with more snow.

Mom went inside ahead of us, unconcerned and oblivious to dad. She was focused to get out of the house as quick as possible. As dad clung to my shoulder we climbed the front stairs. He was winded by the time we reached the front door.

"Thanks," he said.

The house smelt like mothballs and smoke. It was cold and dark, worse than I remembered despite being away for just one night.

I could hear mom as she darted around the rooms above us. She had already started, a reminder to herself that she had gotten her way. She came down the steps, stopped at the base of the stairs.

"I'll be packing the upstairs stuff. You guys sit down and relax."

She didn't wait for a response before she jumped up the steps, two at a time.

"Looks like it's you and me kid," dad said.

"Yeah."

I got the radio, flashlight, and a few blankets from the dining room table. It didn't matter what we listened to as long as it wasn't the echo of mom's steps, a reminder of her excitement for a new life. The radio buffered mom, and kept dad at a distance. She was free to drop an item or slam a door shut. She wouldn't have to worry that dad would call the move off.

That night he stayed quiet, unmoved, and listened to the radio as I fetched him beers and snacks. He had made mom stop at the gas station outside of town to fill up on his essentials. We listened to sports radio. It was good to see dad relax, not getting hyped up on what some idiot fan had to say about his favorite team or complain about what player was overpriced. Every few minutes he'd nod his head in agreement or grunt with disapproval. No yells, no curses, just his best attempt at normal.

Mom stayed upstairs for the rest of the night. She didn't bother to come down for dinner. Our options were limited anyway and with dad hopped up on pain pills his appetite was limited. We ate cold pop tarts and listened to a baseball game. I was amazed at the announcer's nonchalant mention of the eighty-degree temperature and clear, sunny skies like it was no big deal. If he only knew, he'd be grateful.

For that night, while we listened to the game, I understood the appeal. I lost myself in the world that the announcer conveyed. The numbers and names, the technical aspects and the language of the game was something all its own. It had its own rhythm like the jazz records mom used to play. Strike 'em out, throw 'em out, 6-4-3 double play, a groundball with eyes; it all sounded alien. The crowd came alive in the background every so often. A Japanese pitcher faced off against a Dominican batter, a Cuban outfielder threw out a Venezuelan base runner, it was worldly, cultured.

I began to wonder how dad got interested in something like this. The poetry of the game was lost on him no doubt. He didn't care for the announcer's outlandish home run calls, he wanted to hear the score, listen to the crack of the bat, and take in the physical aspects of the contest. It wasn't a modern, unscripted, drama to him. It was a test of wills. Man against man to see who was superior.

Mom had been upstairs for the entire game. Five hours of continuous work. Not one break, not a trip to the kitchen for a glass of water, nothing, not even a flush of the toilet. Dad began to doze off which allowed me a chance to sneak upstairs. I wanted to see how much of our lives could be packed up, concealed, in less than a night.

"Hey."

"You wouldn't believe how much stuff we have taking up space," she said.

Her face was flush, cheeks a rosy hue. Sweat dripped down her cheeks.

"Yeah."

"And this is only our bedroom and bathroom. We still have to get your stuff in order and then all of downstairs. I'm going to need your help. Well, we can talk about that in the morning. Go get some sleep."

Her speech was fast, condensed. She tripped over her own words.

"Goodnight," I said.

She yelled out I love you as if she wanted it on the record one last time. Her motherly kisses on my cheek had phased out over the past few years. We both knew that she held back more for my sake than anything else.

The next morning dad was still sedated. In the same position in his chair, dad called me over.

"You ready?"

I didn't understand. I thought he might still have been half asleep. I just nodded my head. Mom came down the stairs, still dressed in yesterday's clothes.

"Alright, family meeting y'all," dad said.

Mom looked at me and shrugged. It was a comical look. She whispered the words, just let him have his moment.

"You need to help your mom clean out all of this stuff. Figure we bring just the bare essentials."

"Why?" Mom asked.

"We're not gonna go lugging the whole house down the street. We might be in a bind but we're not the Beverly Hillbillies. You guys take care of that stuff and I'll start making some calls. Try to get this place sold."

"How?" I asked.

"I bought a throwaway cell phone awhile back. I'll ask around. There are plenty of people from nearby. Hell, even some of the guys from down at the plant would love to think that they're getting a steal of a property."

Dad chuckled at the thought that he could outwit his buddies. This was what it had come to, what this thing had turned him into.

"You sure we shouldn't get a real estate agent? You know, to make sure we get top dollar?"

Dad laughed at mom as if she were a little child. Mom might've won the war but dad refused to give up on the little battles along the way.

"All they're good for is taking a piece of the pie. That's all the middleman is for. Well, this is my house and I'm getting every red cent out of it!"

"Alright, calm down. I was just asking…"

"Well I was answering. Bad enough we gotta leave but I'm not letting some outsider come in here and take a cut," dad said.

"Okay, okay. But don't jump on the first offer given."

"Ain't no one gonna fleece me out of what's mine. Besides, you're the one that can't wait to get outta here."

Mom grabbed my hand and stomped up the steps. Too much stuff to do to sit and argue with a man whose mind was already made up. It never ceased to amaze me that mom even participated in these arguments given dad's stubbornness.

"Aren't you scared?"

Mom was surprised by my question. She put down the marker that labeled the boxes and sat down on my bed next to me.

"Of what, the move? Sure but it's the best thing for us. We can't stay here."

"I'm worried about what it'll be like where we're going," I said.

"Me too honey, me too."

The moment of silence hung over us. It amplified with each second that passed. Mom sensed my worry. She knew she needed to say more.

"At least the sun will be out. It'll be good, like an adventure. Think of all the new friends you'll make," she said.

I didn't have the heart to tell her that it was impossible for me to make new friends. I wasn't going to admit that the few friends in my life were all losers like me.

W e finished the rest of the upstairs in silence. Mom's optimism faded away as we shivered from one dark room to the next. It was still early in the day. Mom continued at her rapid pace. It forced me to play catch up. For the rest of the day she ran circles around me. Find, fold, pack repeat until all the boxes were full.

We came downstairs sweaty and tired. I heard dad's voice. He was on the phone.

"No, as is. Furniture included. Quick and easy,"

"Let's clean up the kitchen," mom said.

"No, everything is fine. No structural problems, nothing, we don't have power right now because of this storm."

I wondered who was on the other end. If they were somewhere far away, warm and comfortable, using a landline. Mom continued to pack with me between them, somewhere in the middle. I watched mom and listened to dad.

"Well if you're not interested then stop wasting my time. I got a dozen other calls to make. I'm looking to move this fast," he paused for a moment. "Yeah, it's cash only. Everything's in order. Just have to wait for this storm to pass and the electricity to kick back on."

Dad peaked over and winked at me.

"Your dad should've been a used car salesman. He's got a gift for bullshitting."

"He knows what he's doing," I said.

"He sounds like he knows what he's doing. Big difference."

By the time mom cleared the kitchen dad had made another dozen calls. Guys he hadn't spoken with in years, former bosses that he did temp work for on a construction job, other guys from the bar that were better off, he even called his dad's brother. He was desperate and by the end of the night he'd had enough.

"Any luck?" Mom asked.

"Few guys coming over tomorrow. I'll reel one of them in no problem," he said.

He gulped down another can of warm beer from the pantry. Mom went upstairs, this time without a spring in her step. She'd cleared most of the house in less than two days. She was no longer full of energy. It reminded me of when I used to get amped up from too much sugar and then have a bad headache and get grumpy and pass out.

Dad barked at me before bed, mumbled something through the mound of empty cans that had piled up around him.

"Put this sign on the front door. Use a hammer and nail."

CASH ONLY, MUST SELL. BEST OFFER.

Six words that represented how desperate we were, how diminished our lives had become. Because of dad's stubbornness, mom's submissiveness, as well as our lack of money, we had to cut and run. Everyone else around us managed to leave weeks ago. We were like the cockroaches in the aftermath of an atomic bomb.

If the neighborhood wasn't so deserted the sign would've embarrassed me. Humiliated about what we'd become, how cheap and frantic we were. Everything we owned, all of our memories, had turned into nothing more than possessions. Travel light was the orders. Dad left no room for loyalty or sentimentality. We were cloaked in a veil of darkness that allowed us to sneak out of town unnoticed.

Dad was asleep, radio still on - this time national news. I went to bed, tried to convince myself that tomorrow would be better. Our uncertainty was stronger than the storm because we couldn't quantify it, not yet at least.

A bang at our door came the next morning. It was the first time someone had knocked since Bobby said goodbye. Dad rolled off his chair and got to his feet. He struggled to make it to the door before mom and I came downstairs to see about the noise.

"Hey, long time no see Hart!"

"Hey boss, how's it going?"

"I could complain but who'd listen?"

Mom giggled at this. The man came in and took a seat next to dad in the living room. We went into the kitchen. I stayed close, listened in on them.

"You look pretty banged up."

"Nothing a few beers can't fix, right? In fact, you want one?"

"Sure," the man said.

"Hey Wilson grab us two beers."

I handed both of them to dad, scared of the stranger in our house. He smiled at me. He had a big gap where his front teeth should've been and a tattoo on the side of his neck.

"Boss this is my kid Wilson. Wilson, say hi."

"Hey."

"Hey buddy. You're getting big. Might give your old man a run for his money by the time you're done growing."

"Yeah plenty of time for that," dad said. "Go off and let us talk, okay?"

There was silence in the room for a minute as they both had their cans lifted skyward, bottoms up.

"It's good seeing you boss. Bottom line, you interested in this place or is this social?"

"Depends on the price."

"$100,000, given the situation and all."

Dad had paid $125,000 for the house decades ago. At least that's what it said in those papers I found in his closet.

"You're crazy if you think you're getting six figures, what with this storm and everything. Maybe you should wait it out."

"I can't wait it out. What's the highest you can give me? No bullshit or anything straight cash or a check."

The man looked around like he could find some deficiency, something broken to get him a better price.

"Since it's all up front and no paperwork and no waiting and it's me...I could go as high as $75,000."

Dad was quiet for a moment. I didn't know if he was ready to punch him or hug him.

"Hey Wilson, grab the whiskey, we're celebrating!"

They were all smiles. Five minutes and they'd gotten the deal done.

Maybe dad had been in the wrong business all along.

Mom came in after me.

"What's all the ruckus?"

"Hey sweetie, you remember my boss, I worked for him here and there in between the factory? Anyway, he bought the house."

"How much?"

"$75,000," dad said.

Mom stood there. The anger and disappointment on her face said it all.

"What did we talk about last night? Didn't you say you weren't going to take the first deal that came your way?"

Dad got to his feet and leaned on a crutch. He was surprised by mom. That she'd had the confidence to not only force the move but to question the tactics in the process. She was different, unafraid to raise her voice, to cause a scene, to speak up in front of others.

"Don't start with me, not in front of company! If it weren't for you we wouldn't be selling in the first place. It's a solid offer, it's cash, and it's going to a friend. That's the end of it."

Mom walked out of the room.

"Sorry about that."

"No problems. Look I don't want to get you in hot water or anything."

"No, a deal is a deal," dad said.

"Good man. I'll go get my check book from the truck."

He came back with a check cut for $70,000 and an envelope with $5,000 in cash. Dad gave him the necessary paperwork. They shook hands one more time, had another beer, and he was gone. The whole thing, from when mom won the argument until dad had a check in hand, was less than 72 hours.

Mom wanted to get out of here and dad had delivered on his end. Now we had a week to clear out. The final part was on mom. We started with the upstairs. All the boxes that mom had packed were piled by her bed. There were five big ones and a few smaller ones. I noticed that the photos were still on the nightstand and hung up on the wall.

"You're not going to leave the photos?"

"No, honey I'll put them in a box after you get this stuff hauled out to the truck," she said.

Each trip dad grunted louder. The bulk of our stuff was left to me to carry because of his leg. He managed a few at first but lost steam. He dropped the final box outside, almost lost his balance if not for the crutch.

"What the hell is this? We moving a circus or a couple of people?"

Head down and quiet, I shuffled out into the snowy front yard and managed to move everything mom deemed important into the back of the truck. Dad had finished the bottle of whiskey by now. Opened it for a celebration and downed it for a funeral. The house was dead in a way, our memories already collecting dust inside the boxes that were blanketed with a coat of snow.

Mom came down with the photos in one large, open box.

"Any small things like photos and stuff can go in here. But I've only got one more box left," she said.

Dad looked around the living room, at the timeline of our family's slow descent into disappointment. He belched, scratched his belly and went to sleep. He'd laid down the law, made his point. Bad enough he had to move, to concede to someone else, he wasn't about to do it enthusiastically.

Mom went around and grabbed photos that showed us happier, younger, and less cautious. At birthday parties and backyard barbeques. At ball games and day trips to the beach. With each picture mom picked up she lost a bit of herself.

It was too hard to watch, to see her struggle through this. I went up to my room, which was now cleared out, and rested until she had the boxes from downstairs ready to be lugged out to the truck.

The constant noise prevented me from being able to sleep this day away. The fact that I only had a mattress to lie on didn't help. My drawers were empty and so were my closets. Even my stash of dirty magazines was gone.

Curled up on the hard, undersized mattress I began to realize how hard the future was going to be. No school, no house, no job prospects, nothing. We didn't even know where we were going, let alone what to do when we got there.

That night was quiet except for the occasional sound of snow as it hit the roof. Dad slept in his recliner, left the upstairs for us. There was no excitement about the next day, just fear and shame. We had given up, given in to this thing. A temporary weather phenomenon had altered our lives.

W hen I woke up the rest of the boxes were gone. Dad sat up in his chair, sweat glistened off his forehead.

"What are you doing?"

"Good morning to you too," he said.

"Where is everything?"

"Already taken care of. We're all set to go."

"Is mom awake?"

"Stop asking questions. I've got a headache. Get me a beer from the pantry," he said.

"We're all out."

"God fucking dammit! Go wake your mom up so we can get this over with."

Dad's shame had kept him up the entire night. He'd emptied our house of alcohol for the second time in less than a week. Mom came down in her robe and slippers, hair still matted down to one side.

"You do all this?"

"Yeah," dad grunted.

"Now what?"

"Now we leave. Unless there's anything else you think we need to bring with us."

"I'll check around one last time and get changed," she said.

"You're wearing what you've got. Everything else is in the truck and I ain't gonna unpack that thing. It looks like its about to come crumbling down as it is."

"Ugh, fine. Give me a minute."

I followed mom upstairs to take one last look at things. This was it. The finality of the situation had sunk in. The peels on the wall, the faded wallpaper, the faint smell of smoke deep in the wood of my bureau, the outlines of posters taken down. The unfinished hardwoods beneath my cold feet never felt so jagged. No amount of time would be sufficient for me to say goodbye.

Mom lay down on her bed, eyes glued to the dirty ceiling. Tears were in the corner of her eyes. She didn't even try to hide it from me like she usually did.

"You alright?"

"Oh, hey, yeah... I'll be fine once this is all over with. It's just...well, never mind," she said.

"Just what?"

"This was my only home, your only home, except for when I was a girl growing up. Once we got married and had you that was it. This place seemed so big back then. Never thought we could ever get enough stuff to fill it and now, well, now we're tossing it aside."

I sat down next to her on the bed. She still had more that she need ed to say.

"You don't understand sweetie. We were 18 when we moved in. Imagine in a few years you having a place like this to call your own?"

I looked around and thought to myself that it wasn't much to be proud of.

"You'll understand one day. When we first got here I was so worried. Worried about getting along with the neighbors, about being a good wife, a good mother. The thought of cleaning this whole place kept me up those first few nights and now...Now we're practically giving it away for nothing, just folding up shop and leaving," she said.

"But isn't this what you wanted?"

"It's different now that it's happening. It's like I'm saying goodbye to twenty years of my life in the matter of a week and all because of what? A freak snowstorm and your father's medical bills? It doesn't make sense. It's not fair," she said.

I wrapped my arms around her, squeezed her as hard as possible, like she used to do to me. There were no words of comfort.

"I'm sorry for laying all of this on you sweetie," she said.

She wiped away the tears from her face.

"Don't apologize. We're going to be alright mom, trust me."

The sound of a car horn from the street below stopped our conversation. A few short loud bursts were followed by dad's voice. "Let's go! Times wasting!"

I took off my jacket and put it over her robe before we left. Both of us turned around and looked around one last time, took it all in. Just then mom darted into a closet. She came back with a camera.

"Mom, no!"

"Just one, for me honey," she begged.

"Fine."

She snapped a photo of me as I stood at the base of the stairway. It was something to hold onto, to remember this place by. Something to replace the memories of dad's drunken stumbles up those steps to wake up mom late at night after work as he looked for sex or an argument. Mom handed me the Polaroid, dropped the camera, and took a deep breath.

"I want you to keep this. Never let it go, okay. Promise me."

"I will."

We walked out the front door and shut it behind us. Mom rubbed her hands across the worn wood. Dad honked again but mom didn't care. She was on her own schedule now. She wasn't going to be rushed. The next few moments were hers to hold on to, to solidify in her memory.

That day we left our home, my only home for all of my life. We took what we could carry with us. Vagabonds, we had turned into drifters, this thing had turned us into something desperate.

The truck was filled with a lifetime of things and we still had room to spare. It was pathetic. We owned so little and what we did have was so insignificant that it seemed dumb to even move it in the first place. We were in search of a new start but we were bogged down with pieces of our past.

We left without a word. Mom held her tears back and dad was drunk. Shock overcame me, which dulled the pain. Dad used his crutch to hit one of the pedals.

Even now when dad listened to mom and took her directions he still had to put his own twist on it. Make it seem like he was the one in charge. He rushed the process to prove a point, to show her how efficient he could be if he wanted to get things done. Only problem was that this plan wasn't thought out. It was reactionary. We had spent the summer on the defensive, stood our ground the entire time. Now we bolted. We'd gone from stubborn to impulsive in a matter of days.

We trudged through the snow, skated through our deserted neighborhood. By the time we reached the highway, our gateway to a new start, dad already started to curse.

"Shit on a stick. Fuck, fuck, fuck. How could I be so stupid?"

He whipped the truck around. Did a U-turn without hesitation. A box fell off our truck but it didn't matter. He had that look in his eyes. As we approached the house he let out that he had forgotten to clear out his toolshed.

"They're only rusted out tools," mom said.

"What the hell would you know about it? Besides we can get some money for them."

There were bright neon signs all over the house. One was posted on the shed, written with a marker. I brought it to dad, who stood against the truck cigarette between his lips. He looked angry, full of rage, ready to blow.

NO TRESPASSING. PRIVATE PROPERTY. FOR SALE $225,000.

"That fucking weasel! Go get my tools."

The door was locked; a new shiny lock was put on it. I came back empty handed and head down.

"Well?"

"He put a new lock on it," I said.

Dad's plan had backfired. Once again he had tried to outsmart someone and lost. It was a perfect end to this move. Nothing had gone as planned.

"When did he have the time for that? What, was he waiting for us to leave? Give a man a fair deal and he comes and swoops in the minute we're gone and does this!"

"You did sell it to him," I said.

"What'd you say? Don't give me lip. I'm not in the mood. Check the front door in case."

Same result. Mom had poked her head out the window to see about the commotion.

"Just leave it. It's only stuff. We have to get going if we're going to find a place for the night," she said.

"Yeah, yeah," dad said.

He lit another smoke and stood in place, eyes fixed on the house, his house. Dad, in that moment, was hopeless and at the mercy of so many outside forces that I felt sorry for him. I wished I could've told something, anything to be reassured, boost his confidence, but it would've been a lie. He'd been screwed over once again, given a raw deal. We were along for the ride, helpless to assist him in his bad luck.

We got back in the truck and slushed through the snow once again. This time we were gone for good. No more excuses, nothing to hold us back.

As I looked back at our house, on our isolated, dark street I realized that no matter how far dad drove, no matter how hard he pushed down on the accelerator, we wouldn't be able to outrun the harsh flakes that had crystallized and darkened our hearts.

I made a promise to myself that no matter what happened, no matter where we ended up, that dad's present wasn't going to become my future. There was more to life than this scramble to survive. It might have been good enough for my parents but it wouldn't do for me. Mom had tried to turn the ship around, adjust her course in life but it was too late. All of us knew that much but at least she had tried to change our circumstances. Dad had been beaten down and left to accept his role, his existence. Not me, on that trip back through our neighborhood under the darkness of this thing, I told myself that dad's complacency would never be inherited by me.

The reason why dad had become the man he was today was because of me. If it weren't for me he wouldn't have been forced into this role of family man, the provider. That same downfall wouldn't happen to me. The importance of ownership was clear to me. Dad didn't have possession over anything more than a truck full of junk, his family, and a check in his pocket. That wouldn't be me. I wanted, and would have, more.

We got on the freeway, the familiar roads of my childhood now behind us for good. The darkness shifted to light, the snow gave way to grass. The storm melted off our truck with each mile we put between our past and us. The vehicles around us were clean. The sun reflected off them and poked through our windows. Dad turned off the heat and rolled down his window. Mom shed her jacket. I started to sweat.

Things were now visible for the first time in weeks as we moved to the left lane, dad now steady at 80mph. Convertibles with their tops down, drivers with tank tops and sunglasses whizzed alongside us. We were now a part of summer once again.

Mom flipped down her visor to keep the glare out of her eyes. My body began to thaw out, like I'd begun to shed a layer of skin. I rolled up my sleeves, looked at my pale arms and was hopeful, if only for a moment, at the tan that was now once again possible. No longer hidden in the dark, we started to fuss over our appearance. Superficial worries now came back to us, newly prioritized now that we didn't have to contend with that thing anymore.

Soon we hit the state line. Dad continued without a word. The plow was still on the front of the truck. It was up, no longer needed. It served as a reminder of what we were running away from.

Mom reached into the glove box for a map. I caught a glimpse of dad's face in the mirror. He looked determined. He pushed the truck forward.

The hospital bill rushed back to me. It had to be what kept his foot on the gas pedal. I wasn't going to ask him just like mom wasn't going to give him directions. Instead, she looked at the map like it was a novel. She ran her fingers across the folds. It kept her distracted from the reality of the present and the uncertainty of the moment.

The silence was broke when I asked dad where we were going. He took a moment and adjusted his eyes to the rear view mirror and met my eyes, stared deep into them.

"Does it matter?"

"Stop that," mom said to both of us as she turned to face me. "We'll know when we get there."

That's when I realized that we wouldn't know, much like we didn't know about the snow. And no matter where we went, where the snow covered pavement led us, we wouldn't be able to escape that thing. I realized that even if we found a new home, something to stabilize and redefine our lives, a part of all three of us would always live in that dark, damp, cold place.

A week later, while we ate take out Chinese food in a motel four states from our home, a news bulletin broke. The cloud had disappeared, the snow melted, the ice thawed. Gone was the gray blanket that hung over our former home.

The report was brief, only a few minutes, like an afterthought. Not a word was spoken on the how and why of the thing.

The caption on the screen read, The Day The Cloud Stood Still. It sounded like a fairy tale.

Mom put her head down and stared at the cheap, stained rug. Dad grunted. A mouthful of noodles flew back into his container. He got up, cursed, and turned off the television. He got to his feet slowly, still in pain from the fall.

"I'll be back later, I'm going out for a drink."

Neither of us said a word. I hoped that he'd come back by morning. Mom looked indifferent. She was content and warm now that we were out from under that thing.

Other titles available from Pteron Press

Pteron Press Stationary – Notebooks I-V
Timo Tuhkanen – The Dinosaur Suvadeep Das – Manifestation
Max Peake – Absolute Uncertainty
Timo Tuhkanen – Little Yellow Notebook
Timo Tuhkanen – METHETICO
Timo Tuhkanen – Disantropy
Matt Margo – When Empurpled
Jukka-Pekka Kervinen – Osssh

Pteron Press & Pteron Press Music exist only in your imagination and are in no
ways liable for any damages, taxes, or anything, that might be a cause or problem
ever, from reading, existing or becoming.

Contact us for more information:
http://www.pteronpress.weebly.com
00358452795611
pteronpress@gmx.com
pteronpressintern@gmail.com
pteronpress4u@gmail.com

Hernesaarenkatu 11 E 114
00150 Helsinki
Finland

Born in 1986, Patrick Trotti is a writer, editor, and student.

His fiction and poetry have appeared in several literary journals, both online and in print. He's the author of six e-books, published by various small presses. The Day The Cloud Stood Still is his print debut.

His next work is a short story collection that will be coming out in 2015 from Tailwinds Press.

You can find out more about him and his work or from at www.patricktrotti.com.

www.ingramcontent.com/pod-product-compliance
Lightning Source LLC
Chambersburg PA
CBHW020336260626
47156CB00004B/1559